THE SWORD
OF
MERLIN

JARED WOOLF

outskirts
press

Outskirts Press, Inc.
http://www.outskirtspress.com

ISBN: 978-1-9772-1809-4

Outskirts Press and the "OP" logo are trademarks belonging to Outskirts Press, Inc.

PRINTED IN THE UNITED STATES OF AMERICA

CHAPTER 1

Japheth hurried as quickly as he could through the thick pines. He was tired and sweating, having been in the woods all day. Through the pine boughs that wove the heavy canopy overhead, he could just make out a thin wisp of smoke that came from the family homestead. It was nearly sunset, but it was darker than it should have been for this time of day. Over the course of the day, the clouds had moved in and added to the gloom of the situations he had found himself in.

The day had started off like many others. He had helped with the chores around the farm and then headed to the woods with his bow to try to find some fresh meat to supplement his family's diet of grains and preserved vegetables that had been grown the year before.

He was thankful for what they had, but eating the same thing day after day, and month after cold month, was wearing on the entire family. The amount of food they had stored was sufficient for their needs, but at their current rate of use they would be nearly out of food by the time the next growing season came. Finding something to supplement their diet was becoming crucial.

Going into the woods had become more precarious over the last year. Before that time, game was abundant and the number of predators low, but in the last year game had become increasingly scarce, and predators had become more and more numerous. It seemed to his family, like nature was out of balance, there were far more predators than the amount of game would sustain. In addition to there being more predators in the forest, they had gotten more aggressive in their behavior, they were not as easily spooked as they once had been.

The townsfolk had attributed this change to natural cycles in the predator, prey numbers, and most assumed it to be temporary, something that would eventually flow the other way, but Japheth and his family sensed something different, something unnatural.

About an hour into his hunt he came across the fresh tracks of a small deer, which excited him. He had not seen a deer in many months. He noticed he was headed into the wind and decided it would be advantageous to follow the tracks.

After an hour of following the tracks he got his first glimpse of the deer. It was too far away to shoot at, but it seemed to be content and calm. He reasoned that if he was careful, he could sneak up closer and get a decent shot at it.

After much slow, deliberate movement he was close enough to shoot. He quietly nocked an arrow and drew back his bow. That's when he heard the sound of a snapping limb to his left. In an instant the deer had raised its head in alarm, laid eyes on the massive bear, and bolted out of sight through the woods. The bear and Japheth had the same agenda, obtaining a meal of fresh meat. Now that the fleet-footed deer was not an option for the bear, he turned his attention to Japheth. This bear was the largest he had ever seen, by a wide margin. He had most likely just come out of hibernation and was extremely cranky, for which he seemed to blame Japheth.

Immediately Japheth began to climb the nearest tree, which was much too small for the huge bear to climb. After quickly climbing to a height that was out of the bear's reach, he waited.

The bear had reached the base of the tree and was seemingly sizing it up and considering his options. Knowing he was too big to climb the tree, he stood on his hind legs and began to try to push the tree over. Japheth was ready and clung tightly to the tree as it swayed violently back and forth. Unsuccessful in pushing the tree over, or shaking Japheth out, the bear stopped and let out a powerful roar that seemed to shake the forest around him. Japheth used this pause to nock an arrow, take careful aim, and sink an arrow into the bear's shoulder. The bear, visibly aggravated, let out an even more emphatic roar that made the hair on Japheth's neck stand on end. Again, seizing an opportunity, he quickly nocked another arrow and sank it near the first in the massive bear's shoulder.

The bear went berserk. Again he roared, an almost unnatural roar, filled with power and fury. The bear wrapped his huge forelegs around the tree and began trying to pull it out of the ground. The tree was beginning to yield when a third arrow struck the bear in the opposite shoulder. The bear flinched but did not release the tree. Another arrow found its way into the arm of the bear, this caused the bear to release the tree with the wounded arm. As it did a fifth arrow hit the bear alongside the prior one. The bear stopped and dropped on all fours. Japheth sunk another arrow into the bear's hip and then waited to see what it would do next.

He didn't want to waste any more arrows on the bear, he knew he wouldn't be getting them back. The surly bear stomped angrily around the tree, snorting, grunting, and frothing at the mouth. He looked up a Japheth and roared once more, a more subdued sound came from the monstrous bear this time, almost as if he was begrudgingly admitting defeat. After a few moments, the bear headed off roughly in the direction the deer had gone.

When he could no longer see or hear the bear, Japheth climbed down and started swiftly toward home. He had made it about half of the distance when the hair on his neck stood up again.

He slowed to observe the forest around him, and as he looked behind him, he saw multiple sets of reflective eyes in the distance. He knew it was wolves. Japheth quickened his pace for a short time while looking for a tree that would be easy to climb. In a few moments, he saw the ideal tree. He climbed up and waited. As he sat in the tree awaiting the arrival of the wolves, he reasoned that the amount of noise the bear had made must have attracted the attention of the wolves. They had come to investigate and picked up on his scent.

Eventually, the wolves made their way to the tree where Japheth waited. Unlike the bear, they did not seem to be terribly angry, they were almost playful as they watched him in the tree. Being treed by predators rarely happened to Japheth, but it had become more commonplace during the last year.

He nocked an arrow and shot the closest wolf to the tree. The wolf let out a yelp of pain and began trying to gnaw at the arrow in its side. The other wolves began yipping and surrounded the injured one. When the injured wolf fell to the ground, the others pounced. Japheth had known that wolves would attack and eat their own, but he had never witnessed it. The wolves must be extremely hungry to treat one of their own with such savagery.

It was over in moments, and the wolves turned their attention back to Japheth. Their mood had changed. The taste of blood had made them more frenzied and fierce. He decided to try and determine which was the alpha. If he could injure him maybe the others would leave. He looked over the pack but could not conclude which was their leader. In the distance, he spotted a sizable wolf that was refraining from the commotion. In Japheth's experience, the alpha wolf would be at the head of the pack as their leader, so he reasoned that it couldn't be the alpha. He picked another wolf at the base of the tree and shot an arrow. It found it's mark and the wolf yipped in pain. Again, the others waited for it to go down and then converged on it.

Japheth was a running low on arrows, and he hoped that he would not have to use many more on the wolves. If they wouldn't leave, he would probably be spending a cold night in the tree. He had had some run-ins in the past similar to this and had spent the night in a tree a few times. After the second wolf had fallen and been eaten by its companions, the large wolf in the distance let out a long, lonely howl that the other wolves acknowledged, and they headed off toward him.

After waiting for a long while, Japheth climbed down and again headed home as quickly as his tired legs would carry him.

CHAPTER 2

Japheth walked up onto the porch and through the door of their homestead. His mother Abigail greeted him as he entered.

"How was hunting today?" she said cheerfully, even though she could plainly see he had come home empty-handed.

"Well, I was lucky enough just to get back home. I got attacked by a bear, and a pack of wolves."

She smiled, "You have such an imagination Japheth, if you couldn't find anything, no excuses are necessary, we all know you try your best."

He responded, "It's not my imagination I've spent most of the day up a tree."

Abigail's demeanor turned more serious. "Is that true, a bear as well as wolves?" she asked.

"Yes mother, but not to worry there isn't anything in the woods that I can't handle with my bow, but I sure could have used your powers today."

Abigail was a hereditary wizard. Her family records stretched back to the days of Camelot, herself being a direct descendant of Merlin. Through the centuries, the fantastic stories of King Arthur and Merlin had been dismissed by most as myth, but their family records revealed otherwise.

These records contained not only the events that transpired, but detailed genealogy, spells, potions, and most importantly the usage and nature of a most important family heirloom, the sword of Merlin. The sword had never been totally understood by the family. Merlin alone knew how the sword functioned, what it could do, and how to make it do it. After Merlin's imprisonment, the family learned the secrets of the sword by trial and error. The original scabbard for the sword possessed powers of its own, but it had been lost to the family. Aside from its magical powers the sword was a beautiful and effective weapon. The sword always shined as if it was freshly polished and stayed perfectly sharp regardless of its usage.

The family records told of a time when it had been stolen. After not being able to use the swords power, the thief tried to melt it down, only to find that it could not be done. The family had learned that the swords power could only be harnessed by someone who is virtuous, acting in a noble cause. The sword would choose one, and only one at a time, to have access to its tremendous power. All the secrets of the sword had been meticulously kept by this line of Merlin's descendants. Currently, Japheth's grandmother, Tabitha, possessed the sword.

Not long after the time of Merlin, wizards began to be distrusted, then persecuted, then hunted and eradicated. As a result, not many families continued the practice. If not for the sword, it is likely that the trade would have been lost altogether, as far as Japheth's family knew they were the only practicing wizards left. They had kept their family abilities a secret for generations until they had moved to Licentia. They lived a small distance outside of town in a cluster of family cottages. The people of Licentia were somewhat tolerant of the fact that they were wizards.

Their family secret was revealed when a terrible sickness swept through the town. They used spells and their knowledge of potions to help the townspeople recover. At first, everyone was grateful, but it didn't take long for the old prejudices to resurface, and misgivings about their powers became concerning. There were rarely any problems as the family kept to themselves most of the time. Rumors of Merlin's sword had gotten out as well, which may have saved them from more severe persecutions.

Japheth had not taken to his mother's magic trade. He learned his skills with a bow from his father, Eli. Eli had come from a long line of farmers, but he had never been content to sow and reap.

From his childhood, he had a desire for more adventure than a farm could provide. As he grew older, he sought out a way to join the king's army. Eventually, he was successful and became an archer.

He not only learned how to effectively shoot a bow but also how to make them. Through much practice, he developed his own method of shooting that allowed him to shoot extremely fast, and just as accurately as the other archers. He was involved in a few skirmishes, but when called into action he was not in the middle of the battle but stayed back and fired arrows at the enemy usually before the battle began.

This did not satisfy his sense of adventure and he longed to take part in the battles more closely. Eventually, he was granted his wish. During his last battle, the enemy had broken through the lines and some headed toward the archers. As they approached, the archers let their arrows fly and a row of attackers dropped. This was repeated, again and again. They could have held their own, but eventually, they ran out of arrows. The enemy advanced quickly once the arrow supply was exhausted, and the slaughter was horrific.

Nearly all the archers were killed. Eli managed to escape the melee into the safety of the forest. The destruction of so many men cured him of his desire for action in battle.

Knowing that he could not return home, because he would surely be found as a deserter, he headed south. There were rumors of towns that sat just on the boundary of the kingdom that were not loyal, nor antagonistic, to the surrounding competing kingdoms. He saw them as places where someone could go to blend in and disappear. Licentia was one of those towns.

Hungry and tired from his travels, he managed to find Licentia, and the first door he knocked on was that of Abigail's family. He helped with the work on their farm to pay for his room and board. Eventually, he fell in love with Abigail and they were married. He did not find out about the family secret until just before they were married. It only took a few simple displays of their powers to convince him that the family was being truthful. He agreed to keep all this a secret in exchange for keeping his secret of deserting the king's army.

Japheth had been mildly interested in wizardry when he was younger, but upon learning of the oppression that wizards faced, his interest quickly waned.

He spent many hours working alongside his father in the field, learning the best farming practices of the day. He also spent much time practicing with his bow. As the years progressed, he became very proficient in its use. In addition to his bow, he also had spent time learning to make and use throwing knives. During the winter months, there was much time to practice, and he made full use of most of that time mastering archery and knife throwing.

"You'd better get washed up, we're headed to grandma's house this evening to celebrate her seventieth birthday," Abigail instructed.

"Yes mother, is grandma going to read from the family history tonight?" Japheth inquired.

"Yes, I believe she will, that is the tradition," she responded.

Japheth continued with a skeptical question. "Mother, are all those stories real? They seem too far-fetched to have really happened. I know they have been kept by our ancestors, but how do we know they aren't made up?"

Abigail put her sewing down and looked very seriously at Japheth. "I know they don't seem like they can be real, but they are. There are many great lessons to learn from them, and someday you will have stories to add to the records."

He smiled. "How do you know that mother? Have you learned to see into the future now?" he asked sarcastically.

She smiled back, "Just call it a mother's intuition."

Japheth asked excitedly, "Mother, do you think she'll get the sword out?" Japheth had only seen the sword a few times in his life. His grandmother always kept it with her, but seldom drew it from the scabbard.

"Who knows son, if the occasion calls for it, she just might."

It was late afternoon when Japheth's family headed to his grandmother's cottage. As was the tradition for his grandmother's birthday, they ate a family meal, and then gathered around as Tabitha read from the family records and told stories of their ancestors, particularly about the sword.

One of Japheth's younger cousins asked excitedly, "What story will you start with tonight grandmother?"

She replied, "How about we start at the beginning, with your forefather Merlin." She opened an ancient looking fine leather-bound book to the front and took a few moments to study the writing. Tabitha never read directly to the family from the book, she would study the book and then give her summary of what it said. Truth be told she didn't need to look at the book at all, for she had studied it her entire life and knew it all by heart.

"Our family records," she began, "tell of a different story than the one passed down in legends. The oral traditions of King Arthur tell two versions. In one version King Arthur has two magical swords, one he pulls from the stone to pronounce him king, and the other, Excalibur. The other version tells of the swords being one and the same. What if I told you there is truth in both versions, would you believe me?"

There were confused looks and indecisive nodding and shaking of heads among Japheth's younger cousins.

She continued, "King Arthur did pull a sword from the stone, showing he had the right to be king. The other sword in the stories did not belong to King Arthur, but to Merlin, our ancestor. The legend says that he forged the sword himself using dragons fire to perfectly temper the metal and make it indestructible. He named the sword Lux, for such a perfect weapon surely needed a name. After Lux had been forged, Merlin used his extensive knowledge of wizardry to give the sword magical properties. The sword would only respond, magically, to him. He used the sword as an extension of himself, almost becoming one with it. It was able to magnify his powers when used for good. If it was being used for anything less than a noble cause it was simply a magnificent weapon."

"Can we see the sword grandmother?" one of the younger cousins inquired.

Tabitha kindly replied, "Patience my child, if we have time I will show you. Knowing the stories of our family is of more importance than knowing what Lux looks like." She continued, "After Merlin was imprisoned, Lux was a bit of a mystery to the family. He had been very secretive about how Lux worked, and what it could do. The family believed that this is because he was somewhat unsure about the capability of the sword.

"Through trial and error, the family has pieced together many of the swords secrets. One ancestor, William, figured out the spell to harness lightning. Dragons were surrounding him in a battle for our ancestral lands against some other, dark, wizards. The situation did not look good for William and those that fought alongside him. The dragons began to circle as the wizards advanced on them. It was out of desperation that he tried the spell and BOOM came the lightning!" Tabitha bellowed as she lunged at the children. They all jumped at their grandmother's words.

Tabitha went on excitedly describing other outlandish stories about the sword. The stories included tales of bravery and valor, dark wizards and dragons, and other mythical creatures. One story included an ancestor using the sword in battle. He became strengthened by the sword and was able to move with exceptional agility and speed. Fast enough, as the legend is recorded, to catch an arrow in its flight.

At other times, Lux was able to cut through anything with no resistance. The book states that Lux cut through a tree as wide as a man with one stroke. It also cut cleanly through stone in another tale.

She also told of when Lux was drawn from its scabbard and it blinded the enemies of their family.

The entire family was getting wrapped up in the stories, even Japheth who remained skeptical of their truthfulness, when one of the children asked, "Grandmother, have you ever had to use the sword?"

Tabitha's demeanor changed from excitement to one of solemnity. "Yes, I have," she replied.

"When?" the children askedeagerly. "Can you tell us your story?"

"I will," she said. Even though Japheth was skeptical, this change in his grandmother caught his attention and he longed to hear her story.

"I received the sword when I was fifteen years of age from my father. I did not fully believe the family stories of the sword. It was given to me by my father, with the admonition to study the family records and become familiar with what the sword could and would do. I did not study much in the first year I had Lux, and the day arrived when I needed to know how to use it, but I was unprepared. I had gone deeper into the forest than normal gathering berries. I was just collecting the last of what I needed to fill my basket when something inside me became very anxious. I looked around but could not see anything out of the ordinary. I felt uneasy and decided to hurry home.

"Just as I headed towards home, I caught a blur moving out of the corner of my eye. As I looked to see what it was my heart dropped, it was wolves."

Some of the children audibly gasped. "I dropped my basket and began screaming and running for home. I was sure I wasn't going to make it. I was too far into the forest. I ran as fast as my feet would carry me. I glanced back and could see the wolves coming. I decided to climb a tree. I had just gotten out of the wolves reach when I heard my father call for me. His yells attracted the wolves attention.

"They started towards him, but he wasn't focused on them, he was focused on finding me. I yelled to him and waved my arms to try to show him I was okay, but he didn't notice. As the wolves approached, he was able to hold them off well. Over the years he had become accustomed to having Lux with him, and since I now had it, he was not as sharp as he normally would have been with his spells. As he fended them off, I was beginning to grow hopeful that he would be alright. I drew Lux from its scabbard and tried to think of something that I could do to help, my mind was blank because I hadn't prepared.

"That's when I noticed that one of the wolves had circled around behind him undetected. He sneaked up on my father, attacking him from behind. I couldn't do anything but watch and scream.

"There were any number of things that I could have done with the sword to help my father if I knew how, but because I was not ready, I was not able to help him." Tabitha fought hard to keep her emotions in check as she continued.

"After the wolves killed my father, a rage grew inside me and I wanted to kill every one of them. My mind recalled the spell for fire, ignis. Not being knowledgeable about the sword, I pointed it at the wolves and yelled 'ignis!' Nothing happened. I tried again. Again, nothing happened.

"I stayed in the tree for a time weeping for my father and hating the wolves. When they had left, I made my way home to tell the rest of my family what had happened. It was a very difficult time for our family. I asked my mother why the sword would not work for me. She explained that I was trying to use it in hatred, which is not a righteous cause. It may be justifiable, but it is not righteous.

"From that day forward, I promised myself that I would know everything in our family book by heart so that if I needed to use the sword again I could."

A solemn feeling had fallen over the family as they listened to Tabitha. Japheth felt sick to his stomach as he thought about what his grandmother had lived with all her years. He then realized that his grandmother had said she had used the sword, but in the story, she had not actually used it.

"Grandmother," Japheth said reverently. Tabitha was brought back from her thoughts with a slight shaking of her head, "but when did you use the sword?"

A small, melancholy smile crossed her face as she said, "I'm glad you reminded me, Japheth. Years later, when I had a family of my own, we were running low on some of the ingredients we needed for some of our potions, so we headed to the mountains to get them. We were about halfway up the mountain when there was a great earthquake. There was a thunderous noise and considerable shaking for what like seemed an hour.

"When the ground finally stopped, the thunder did not cease. I looked up at the mountain and could see a broad rockslide coming down the mountain, and we were in its path. At first, I panicked and looked for somewhere to find shelter from the slide, none of the spells known to our family could stop something as powerful as this massive rockslide. I briefly scanned the surrounding area, but obviously could not find anything suitable. Then I remembered the sword.

"Instinctively I moved between my family and the rockslide, I pulled Lux from its scabbard, held it out in front of me and yelled 'clipeum!', which is the spell for..." she was looking at and motioning to her grandchildren, waiting for one of them to fill in the blank.

One of the older grandchildren said, "Shield!"

Tabitha smiled, "Correct," she said pointing to the child, then continued, "From out of the sword came a kind of nearly transparent, blue light that formed a large disc in front of my family. As the rockslide hit the light it was deflected around us and my family was kept safe. Now the clipeum spell is nowhere near strong enough to withstand a rockslide, so why were we not buried?"

"Because you were protecting your family," came the answer from the children.

"That's right, how were we protected?" she asked.

"Because your powers were magnified?" an older child said, unsure of his answer.

"Correct again, you children are so wise."

"Is that the only time you've used the sword?" asked a grandchild.

"Luckily, yes it is. As the generations have come and gone there has been less and less of a need to use the sword. I believe the world we live in is becoming more civilized and maybe one day we may not need it at all. Until then it is important to always be prepared for the worst, even if it never happens."

"Can we see the sword now Grandma?" the grandchildren asked excitedly.

"Yes, I suppose there's time before you go home." With that,

Tabitha pulled out the sword and scabbard, which had been concealed in a fold of her dress. The children's eyes went wide as they beheld the sword that so much of their family stories revolved around.

"Take it out Grandma!" they implored. Tabitha grabbed the sword by the grip and slowly withdrew it from the scabbard. Its perfectly polished blade gleamed in the firelight. The children began to enthusiastically rehearse the stories they had just heard to one another while pointing to the sword.

Amidst the excitement, one of the children asked, "May I hold it?"

Tabitha smiled gently and replied, "No, I think it best to let Grandma hold it, I wouldn't want anyone to get hurt."

"Grandmother make it do something!" came another request.

"That's not how it works, it can only be magical if it's involved in performing a noble or virtuous task." There was a small amount of collective disappointment from the group of children, but not enough to completely calm the buzz that the sword had created. Tabitha continued to hold the sword so the grandchildren could see and admire it. Japheth noticed as she did, her facial expression went from one of happiness to thoughtfulness and then to total concentration.

Abigail asked, "Mother, is everything alright?" Tabitha completely ignored her question.

Abigail repeated a bit more earnestly, "Mother, what's the trouble?" Once more she was ignored. Abigail crossed the floor, meandering her way through the children. When she reached her mother, she put her hand on her shoulder which snapped Tabitha back to reality. "Mother, are you alright?"

"Yes, yes I am dear, sorry about that. I was just thinking about something." She deliberately looked across the room and made eye contact with Japheth, then continued without breaking her gaze.

"Would you and your family please stay after everyone has left? I'd like to talk to you about something."

"Of course mother."

After everyone had left Tabitha's cottage she turned to Abigail's family and spoke. "Tonight something happened to me that I have been waiting for a good many years to happen. I have gotten long in the tooth, and I was getting apprehensive about who should carry the sword after me. After telling the family stories tonight I have come to know who the sword is to be passed on to." She again retrieved the sword, hidden amongst her dress, walked across the room and stood in front of Japheth.

"I have gotten the indisputable impression that I am to give the sword to you Japheth." The young man stood perplexed about what his grandmother had just told him. In his mind, he was running through all the reasons why he could not be the one to have the sword. He had been skeptical of the truthfulness of his family's stories. He was more interested in the skills that his father possessed than those of his mother and her family. He knew very little of wizardry as he had not studied it since he was a small child.

"Grandmother, I cannot possibly be the one, you must be mistaken," he stammered.

"No, I'm quite sure It's you," she returned.

"I can't, I mean I don't know spells, or potions, or..."

He was cut off by his kindly grandmother, "That doesn't matter Japheth, the sword chooses whom it will. We may not understand why, we just must understand that's how it is. I felt very much like you when my father told me I was the next. He was just outside the physical prime of his life, but he was just entering his intellectual prime, where his wisdom and experience would prove most valuable in using the powers of the sword. It made no sense for him to give it up at that time, but he did. Now, just as I was reluctant to take it, you must."

She held the sword out in front of Japheth. "You must take it and learn all you can about it, and how it works. That is one of the responsibilities of carrying the sword, to continue to unlock it's secrets so that future generations may use that knowledge to protect our family, and all that is good."

Japheth broke eye contact with Tabitha and looked down. "Grandmother, I can't..."

Again he was interrupted, "You must Japheth. Call it your destiny, your mission, your calling or what you will, but it is your responsibility to bear."

Japheth looked up at his father. Eli looked uncertain. He had embraced the fact that his wife and her family were wizards, but he was worried about what type of persecution would come upon his eldest son for not only being known as a wizard but also as the one that carried the sword. Japheth could sense his father's apprehension about what was being asked of him. He moved his gaze from his father to his mother.

Abigail was smiling, as she usually did. With a slight nod of her head, she motioned for him to take the sword. "Go ahead Japheth, take it." He looked back to his father as if asking for permission. Eli hesitated for a moment and then gave an almost imperceptible nod of his head as he closed his eyes. Japheth looked back to his grandmother and passively took the sword.

"Good," she said happily, "now we can really begin your study of wizardry and the family secrets."

"Family secrets?" Japheth asked.

Tabitha grinned, "Yes, you don't think that I share all there is to know during the stories on my birthdays do you? There are many things contained in the book that are both delightful and disturbing that the one who wields the sword must know."

"Like what?" he asked.

"Like our ancestor William that called down lightning." Japheth looked confused. She continued, "Sure, he called down lightning that rid our land of the dark wizards and dragons, but it also killed him. Something that powerful cannot be controlled, even by the most powerful wizard, even with the aid of the sword. The book contains a list of all spells that do and don't work with the sword. Some spells only work with the aide of the sword. There is an enormous amount of information to learn, but if you're dedicated you can get through it all in about a decade or so," she said jokingly.

Eli interjected, "I still need help with the farm, and I'd like him to continue practicing with his bow."

Abigail replied, "Yes, of course, he will still help his father, and make time for his bow. Isn't that correct Japheth?"

"Yes, I will only come to grandmother's once my responsibilities at home are fulfilled."

Tabitha spoke directly to Japheth, "That's fine, but you must make time to study. If you do not, I fear that you may regret it as I have these many years. You must be ready at all times to know what you must do."

CHAPTER 3

Japheth had difficulty falling asleep that night. His mind raced through the stories he had heard from his grandmother, and he fantasized of all the things that could be in the book. When sleep did come it was restless. It seemed each time he fell asleep his dreams were filled with dark wizards, dragons, talking bears, wolves, and all other manner of unnatural beasts bent on his destruction. What all the dreams held in common was his futility in using the sword, which now lay beside him in his bed. After his grandmother had given him the sword, she admonished him to always keep it within his reach.

The next morning was both welcomed and dreaded by Japheth. Welcomed because he was not getting any rest when he did sleep due to his nightmares, but dreaded because he awoke enervated from the night before. He knew he still had a full day of chores, and practice with his bow before heading to his grandmother's house to begin his study. The thought of having access to his ancestral book did give him enough gumption to drag himself out of bed and begin his work.

He hustled through his chores, careful to do them correctly. His father would be paying particular attention to how his chores were completed. Eli would not let the quality of Japheth's work be diminished simply because he had somewhere else to go. After completing his chores, he spent some time practicing with his bow, although not as much as usual, then he hurried to his grandmother's house. Tabitha was outside working the dirt in her garden when Japheth arrived.

"Hello Japheth, did you sleep well?" she asked with a smile.

"No, I can't say that I did. I couldn't keep my mind from thinking about all the things you talked about, and when I could sleep, I had nightmares about some of the other things you told me."

"I thought that would be the case, it is a lot to reflect on," she said.

Tabitha rose from the ground and brushed the debris from her dress. "Are you ready to begin your study?"

"I'm as ready as I can be," Japheth replied. "I'm not sure what it is going to take, so I guess it's just best to begin."

"Did you bring Lux?" Tabitha inquired.

"Of course I did grandmother, you told me never to let it leave me."

"Good, you'll do well to always follow that advice," she replied.

Tabitha and Japheth went into his grandmother's house. Japheth sat down at the table and Tabitha went into a back room and brought out the family book.

"Japheth, there are many inspiring, and enlightening records in this book. They will help you see the good in the world and give you much hope for the future. There are stories of those in our family, and out of it, that have stood up for what is right, and that have sacrificed to help others.

"There are also dark, evil records in this book. Stories that show the worst that mankind is capable of. Some people will do worse things than you can imagine in order to get power, seek revenge, or gain control over others. There is a natural balance that exists in the world between these two forces. It is vitally important that you study this book to help you learn to recognize the difference and be ready to fight for that which is right. Those stories are just as important to know as the information in the book about Lux. I don't want to scare you, but after you have read those things, your nightmares from last night may seem mild in comparison."

"Why do I need to know those things grandmother?" asked Japheth. "Haven't you just explained it to me?"

His grandmother replied, "Yes I have, but in order for you to better understand, you need to read of those things that have happened by those who experienced or witnessed them. You have lived a somewhat sheltered life on your farm, and you need to know what the rest of man's world can be like. You are very skilled at surviving on your own in nature, but man can be a more terrible beast than anything else you could possibly encounter in the forest."

With that, they began reading the book together. The first part of the book contained potion recipes, complete with a list of ingredients, and instructions on how to correctly concoct each one. The next portion of the book was the list of spells. There were many, many pages of the common spells of wizardry, followed by a significantly shorter list of spells that were known to be enhanced using Lux. Following that was the pieced together history of what was understood of the sword, and some of the powers it had to offer. Many of these had been evident in the stories that Tabitha had told, but not all. What was confusing to Japheth was the fact that it was not understood how to get Lux to do a good many of the things that it could do and had done in the past. There was still much mystery about how it worked. Japheth's mind reflected on the story about how an ancestor received extreme quickness and agility, but it was not known how to harness that power.

Subsequently, there was the shortest list of all, which was a list of spells that were known to work only when the appointed wizard was wielding Lux. These spells where clearly the most powerful in the book. A few of the spells caught Japheth's attention. How to call down lightning, fulgur, was on the list. A spell that would contain a dragon's fire, captis, and another, exsolvo, that would shoot it back. At this point, Japheth turned to Tabitha with a question.

"Grandmother, are there really such things as dragons?"

"Yes, yes there are," she responded. "I have not seen any in my lifetime, but my grandfather spoke of seeing one when he was just a small boy."

Japheth followed with, "Where have they gone?"

"That I don't know. They were hunted extensively, much like wizards because they couldn't be controlled, I suppose they are extinct, or maybe in hiding like us," she said with a smile.

"If they are extinct, I presume I do not need to spend time learning spells to combat them, it would just be a waste of time," Japheth said.

Tabitha responded thoughtfully, "Perhaps, but perhaps it would be best to learn them too, just in case. It is always better to be over prepared than under prepared. After all, it can take hundreds of years for dragons to reach maturity."

The final section of the book was the location of the stories of note from the days of Merlin, down to his grandmother's experience of saving her family on the mountain. Japheth paused before he began reading. He was excited to learn of the stories of bravery and valor, but also apprehensive, almost scared to read of the negative events of the past.

"I don't know if I can read on, I feel a little nervous, can we start here tomorrow?" Japheth inquired of his grandmother.

She returned, "I guess it would be okay, you have covered a lot of information today. In fact, if you'd like to wait on the last section, we could go over the beginning parts of the book again tomorrow."

"I would prefer that, in fact, I would like to wait until I stop having nightmares. If not, I think I'll just give up on sleeping," he said.

"That should be fine, I don't want you to wait too long though, it is nearly as important to know those stories as it is to know the rest of the book."

Japheth headed home with a lot of information to sort through. Between the potions, spells, and Lux's abilities, his mind felt crowded with all the new material that he would need to eventually know.

He got home in the early evening and was met by his father.

"Well son, how did it go?" Eli asked.

"It was good, we covered a lot for the first day, I feel a little overwhelmed."

"Come hunting with me in the forest so we can talk," urged Eli. Japheth nodded his head, grabbed his bow, and father and son moved into the forest.

"Japheth, are you sure this is something you want to do? I want you to think long and hard before immersing yourself into this."

Japheth answered, "I think so father, I know I haven't shown too much interest for mother's skills in the past, but I feel like grandmother has put a great deal of trust in me, and I don't want that trust to be misplaced. I am a little unsure, but after today I think I am equal to the task."

Eli took a slow breath and said, "I don't really know how to say this, so I'll just say it. I have misgivings about you taking on this responsibility. In most places, wizardry is not tolerated, and I get the feeling we won't be tolerated here forever either. If you take on the mantel as the one that carries the sword, I'm afraid you could be looked at as one to make an example of, and I fear for your safety and the safety of our family.

"I have never tried to interfere with the ways of your mother's family or their traditions, but I can't ignore this inclination, and I feel it is my responsibility as your father to let you know the impressions I have about it. I want you to at least consider this when making your decision."

Father and son continued moving further into the forest lengthening their conversation without really looking for game. This outing was not about hunting, but more of a chance to talk things over. Their discussion had distracted them from noticing how late in the day it had become. The evening sun was just beginning to set when they realized how deep they had progressed into the forest, and how quickly the evening would become night.

"We'd better be heading for home, who knows what we might find in this forest after dark," Eli said somewhat cautiously to his son.

Japheth asked, "Wouldn't it just be the same things we would find during the day?"

"Maybe, but the forest doesn't seem to be the same these days. The animals are acting strangely, and your mother seems to think that it may be something other than the ordinary changes of nature. Your grandmother had said something about this being similar to some story in her book." As Eli finished speaking, they both heard the crack of fallen twigs some distance behind them.

Eli was the first to notice the reflective eyes of a wolf. While gesturing with his head he said to his son, "Look there in the underbrush between those two big pines." Japheth quickly spotted the glowing eyes as well.

"Start to head towards home, quickly, but don't run," Eli instructed his son.

They started moving swiftly for home always keeping an eye on the wolf. It followed them at a distance as they fled. The wolf always stayed concealed in the brush and thick trees so that they could never get a good look at it. When they were still quite a ways from home the wolf let out the same long, lonely howl that Japheth had heard the previous day. As the wolf howled, Japheth turned to take a look at it. As he laid eyes on it, his body seemed to tense, it appeared to be the same wolf he had seen the day before. Just as the howl ended it was answered by other lonely howls in what seemed like every direction in the forest. Eli looked at his son and in a low calm voice said, "Run."

Eli and Japheth darted through the forest. As they did both men retrieved their bows and pulled arrows from their quivers. As they ran, they could see glimpses of blurry figures pursuing them through the timber. As the figures began to converge on them Eli looked at Japheth and said, "On my word stop and fire." Japheth nodded and Eli barked, "Now!"

In unison father and son skidded to a stop, bows drawn, and began firing. Japheth prided himself on not just being an accurate shot, but also quick. Before he could get his first shot off, he had heard a painful yelp from two wolves that his father must have hit. His first shot was true, as was his second. As he released his third arrow, which found its target, he had subconsciously counted that his father had downed five of the beasts. His thoughts briefly centered on how much faster his father must be with a bow, and he desired to see him in action.

Eli barked again, "Run!"

Again, the two bolted through the woods. They had downed the bulk of the wolves that had merged on them. Japheth looked over his shoulder to see the downed wolves being attacked and eaten by the others.

"That should buy us some time, don't slow down," Eli ordered his son.

They repeated this process multiple times as they attempted to make their way home. Downing a few wolves at a time would allow them a short head start on the wolves that followed. Japheth noticed his father was slowing a bit but was just as good with his bow when they stopped. He began to think that they would make it home, but he failed to realize that with each stop his father was firing more arrows than he was. He had six arrows remaining while his father had only one. Both knew that they would have to make one more stop before they could get to their home.

They were nearly to the clearing that lead to their homestead when Japheth heard his father. "Japheth give me your arrows," he demanded as they ran.

Japheth looked over to see that his father had only one arrow. Japheth's mind quickly flashed through his options and he realized his father would take the arrows and insist that he continue home.

"I won't leave you behind," Japheth returned.

"There are arrows in a quiver on the porch. Give me your arrows, run ahead, get them and come back," Eli instructed his son.

Japheth grabbed his arrows and handed them to his father. With that, he dashed ahead. As he neared the porch, he heard the familiar yelping of injured wolves. He reasoned that his father had stopped and was trying to hold the wolves at bay until he could return. As he neared the porch his eyes lit on the quiver, but it was devoid of arrows.

His stomach dropped as he realized his father had most likely known there were no arrows in the quiver, he was simply holding the wolves off so that Japheth could get home safely. Japheth whirled to see his father shoot the last of his arrows, drop his bow, and draw his sword. As the wolves continued to emerge from the forest Japheth began sprinting back towards his father.

Eli caught a glimpse of Japheth returning and shouted, "No

Japeth get back home!" His plea was in vain. In the instant that Japeth had realized what his father's plan was, he had determined to go back and help his father, most likely at the cost of his own life.

As he ran, he put his hand on the grip of Lux and his mind raced frantically to recall some spell that could help. His mind was blank. He could not recall a single one. All he could focus on was getting to his father before it was too late.

He could see the wolves continuing to converge on his father and his heart sank with dread. He would be too late, but that would not stop him. No matter the outcome he would share his father's fate. In desperation, he drew the sword and yelled with as much vigor as he could muster. As he did his entire body began to tingle, and from his vantage point, everything but himself seemed to slow down.

His mind briefly recalled a story from the night before about an ancestor that temporarily received tremendous speed and agility during battle. He reasoned that this is what was happening now. Just an instant before, he was sure he was too far away to aid his father, but now it seemed less certain. As he neared the chaos, he saw a wolf attempting to circle behind his father that had gone unnoticed. Just as the wolf was about to pounce, Japeth dove forward bringing the sword down, cutting the wolf in two. Japeth hit the ground, rolled, and was back on his feet in an instant.

The ensuing battle was a blur. All Japeth could see were what seemed like an endless flow of claws and fangs all seemingly bent on his and his father's demise. He cut and slashed with Lux, with everything still moving in slow motion.

He glanced back at his father and saw that a wolf had knocked him over and was now on top of him. Japeth burst to his father's side and kicked the wolf with all the strength he could muster, sending the wolf soaring through the air. He quickly reached down and grabbed his father under his arm and yanked upward. He not only lifted his father to his feet, but lifted him off his feet. With his father's arm now wounded he knew he must do more if they were to survive.

Again, he attempted to recall some spell that could assist them, when into his mind entered the story about his grandmother wanting to slay the wolves that had killed her father and the spell she had used was ignis. Instinctively Japheth clenched Lux in his right hand, held out his left, pointing it at the wolves and yelled, "Ignis!"

A ball of flame much larger than any he had seen his family use jumped from his hand. He watched as it bore down on the approaching wolves. When the broad ball of fire hit the ground, it exploded out and engulf the incoming wolves. There was a mingling of painful yelps, and fear filled barks as the wolves, some of them aflame, retreated towards the forest.

Japheth spun around to the other side of his wounded father to see the remainder of the wolves withdrawing to the forest as well. As the commotion ceased, he again heard the lonely howl of a wolf, seemingly beckoning his companions to join him in the safety of the forest.

When all was calm Japheth situated Lux back into his scabbard. With the mighty sword resting firmly at his side, he released his grip. As he did a wave of exhaustion washed over him, causing him to stumble and nearly faint.

Eli rushed to his side while holding his wounded arm. "Japheth are you alright?"

Japheth stood looking at the ground, and taking a moment to steady himself he answered, "Yes father, I think I'm alright." After a few more moments Japheth looked up at his father to see a look of bewilderment on his face.

"Japheth, son, what did you just do?"

CHAPTER 4

Eli and Japheth struggled towards home. The noise from the commotion had gotten the attention of the entire family and they rushed to help.

"What happened?" Abigail asked Eli.

"We got attacked by wolves," he answered.

"How many?" she queried.

Eli responded, "Too many to count, it started deep in the forest and they followed us relentlessly. That was not normal behavior, not even from hungry wolves." He shot Abigail a concerned glance while slightly shaking his head. Tabitha caught the subtle communication between the two and interjected. "It seems as if our suspicions are confirmed then."

Abigail nodded her head and said, "Yes, I believe so."

Japheth was puzzled at their conversation and inquired, "What are you talking about?" As he spoke, he stumbled and fell.

Abigail helped him to his feet and said, "I will inform you of our concerns once you are in better shape to hear them. You need rest and your father's arm needs attention."

The two weary men were whisked into the house and Japheth was made to get into bed while Eli's arm was tended to at the table. Japheth wanted to protest but was too fatigued to do so. In his weary state, he quickly fell asleep.

Japheth awoke the next morning feeling renewed. He could tell by the sunlight streaming into his room that he had slept longer than usual. He rose, dressed, and went outside to begin his chores. He must have slept much longer than he had guessed, as all the daily chores were already completed. He looked around but could not see any of his family around the house or barn. Given the previous day's events, he surmised they all must be at his grandmother's house. As he opened the door to Tabitha's home, he saw all the adults sitting around the table. He found the seriousness of their expressions troubling. Tabitha's demeanor quickly changed to one of happiness and excitement. She smiled at Japheth with a gleam in her eye and asked, "How do you feel this morning, hero?" Japheth was caught off guard at her compliment. He hesitated a moment, not sure of what to say.

"Well?" Abigail prodded.

"I feel great, considering what happened, and also a little hungry," he said with a smile.

Tabitha hopped to her feet. "Of course, you didn't get any supper last night. You could surely use something to eat."

"Mother," Abigail interrupted, "you stay there, I'll find Japheth something for breakfast." Abigail pulled a bowl from the cupboard and filled it with cold porridge from the pot. She moved her hand across the open bowl while softly muttering a few words too quietly to be heard. Immediately the porridge began to steam. She then handed the bowl of hot porridge to Japheth and motioned for him to listen to the conversation the adults were having at the table.

As Japheth moved nearer the table the talking ceased. Tabitha took the lead. "So Japheth, tell us everything that happened."

He responded, "I don't know for sure, I..."

"Japheth, that will not do," she interrupted, "we must know every detail of what happened. What you saw, sensed, and thought. Take a few moments to think if you need to."

Japheth stopped and gathered his thoughts before beginning. He rehearsed the entire ordeal from beginning to end, from the time his father met him at their home until he fell asleep that night. He tried to be meticulous in every detail, so the story took a great deal of time to tell.

When he had finished Tabitha asked, "Is there anything else, anything at all that you have left out?"

"No grandmother, that's everything."

"Good," she said. "Now I want you to write it all down in the book, every detail that you have told us today."

Japheth had not noticed but the family book was sitting in the middle of the table, opened to the very back. The final page alone was blank. A chair was cleared for Japheth and the book was set in front of him, along with a writing quill and bottle of ink.

Japheth began writing, but soon stopped to ask a question, "What shall I do when the page is full?"

Tabitha answered, "When you get to that point let me know, and I'll show you."

Japheth nodded and went back to writing, not really understanding her answer. When he had filled the paper he again asked, "What do I do now that the paper is filled?"

Tabitha, walking over to Japheth and with a twinkle in her eye said, "Watch."

She closed the book and waited briefly before reopening it to the back. Much to Japheth's surprise, the last page in the book was once again blank. He looked at the preceding page and it contained all his writing. He looked up at his grandmother with a gleeful smile and asked, "How is this done?"

Tabitha shrugged her shoulders and said, "I don't know, it just happens. Each time the book is closed when it is full, a clean page appears in the back." The explanation was both intriguing and satisfying to Japheth. He picked up the quill and began writing again. He needed to repeat the process several more times to get his entire story into the book. When he finished, he closed the book and got up to find the adults.

They had taken their discussion outside. As Japheth stepped onto the porch the talking came to a halt. After a few moments of silence, Japheth asked, "Now can you tell me what you think is going on with the wolves?"

Eli was the first to speak. "As you know there is a natural ebb and flow of animal populations in relation to one another. This relationship has been out of balance for a while, not long enough to raise serious suspicions, but it is noticeable. That alone is no need for concern, but there is something else. For quite some time now the animals in the forest have been acting strangely, the predators in particular."

"I know, I have been in the forest and have noticed it firsthand. I have also overheard some of your discussions when you have spoken of those things, but why is this happening?" Japheth asked once again.

Abigail explained, "There are similar stories in the family book. Long ago a dark wizard was attempting to use animals to do his bidding. Initially, he was somewhat successful but was not consistent enough to be much of a menace. A few years later another wizard, his apprentice, took what he had done and advanced it to gain better, more complete control. He was very successful in using some of the more common animals to obey his commands. This did give him some degree of power, but he became a legitimate threat to humanity when he was able to begin to control other creatures such as trolls and dragons.

"Once he reached this point, he became so engrossed in his own power that he couldn't get enough. He began striving to conquer not just towns and villages but entire kingdoms. Eventually, multiple empires banded together to defeat him. Had he not let his lust for power consume him, he very well could not have been beaten."

Japheth took a moment to think. "Is that what you believe is happening?"

Tabitha answered, "There are many similarities. After what happened yesterday it does seem to confirm our suspicions, but we can't be sure. It is best to prepare for that possibility, and also to gather any information we can on where this could be coming from. Until we find out more, I would suggest that we do not travel into the forest unless absolutely necessary, and if we do, always in groups of two or more."

Japheth asked, "How do we prepare for something like this?"

"In a way, we are always preparing for it," Eli remarked. "You and I practicing with our bows. The rest of the family staying sharp with their spells and potions. Being prepared is just part of the way we live. We just need to make sure we heighten our awareness and keep our ears open for any information that might be useful."

"And," Tabitha interrupted, motioning towards Japheth, "making sure the one who wields Lux is ready for all situations."

Eli continued, "After seeing exactly how that sword can help, I think it would be best to make that your focus for now Japheth."

Japheth nodded, "I think you are right." He turned to look at Tabitha. "Grandmother I think I should read the stories in the book as well. I don't think it can be any more shocking than what happened yesterday."

The rest of the adults left Tabitha's cottage and again the book was set in front of Japheth. He turned to the section of the book that contained the stories he had not read the previous day. Before he began reading, he stopped to ask a question.

"I was thinking about your story when the wolves got your father. I understand that Lux will only work if your intentions are good, but why didn't your ignis spell work? You should be able to use that spell without Lux, isn't that correct?"

Tabitha nodded her head and responded, "Yes, that is correct. The ignis spell has nothing to do with Lux. However, Lux will not allow the chosen wielder to use magic for an unjust cause. That is why you were able to use the ignis spell to defend your father and yourself, and I was not able to use it. It will be vitally important in the future that you have only the best, pure motives for your actions, otherwise you will be not only left to your own strength, but you will be stripped of any magic you may know how to use."

The weight of his grandmother's words troubled Japheth. He was unsure if he would always be able to have pure motives to justify his actions, he knew he certainly hadn't in the past.

As he read the stories in the book he was astonished at the heroic, selfless deeds contained within its pages. He was also deeply disturbed by the shockingly horrendous acts that men would do to each other. He was wrong in his assumption that nothing in the book could be as disturbing as his latest experience. He did not get through all the stories before the sun was beginning to set. His grandmother sat beside him and put a hand on his shoulder. "Japheth, I think it would be best if you started for home."

With a sick feeling in the pit of his stomach Japheth nodded and said, "I think you're right," then he asked, "when will I get the book?"

Tabitha looked at him sweetly and said, "When I pass on." Her answer startled Japheth and she continued, "It is now my job to teach you all that I can while I am here."

"I guess I'd never thought about life without you around," Japheth said.

"Well you'd better start, once the sword has been passed on, the preceding bearer is nearly at the end of their time in this sphere," she said.

Japheth looked at her with sadness on his face and asked, "Why is that?"

She replied, "I don't know, but that has been the pattern down through the ages, and I suspect that is the way it will always be."

Japheth walked the short distance to his house, his mind overwhelmed with the knowledge he had absorbed throughout the day. The animals being under someone, or something's control, all the awful things that had been recorded in the book, and the fact that his grandmother may not be with them for very much longer had put Japheth in a melancholy mood. He briefly confided in his parents about what had transpired at his grandmother's house before heading off to bed, where his dreams where sure to be a spontaneous mixture of all that he had learned that day.

When Japheth laid down, he had no intention of falling asleep. He knew his entire night was going to be filled with nightmares, and he figured it was better for him to stay awake through the night. He was mostly correct. He slept very little and when he did, it was restless and alarming. He woke several times in a cold sweat, sometimes gasping for air, or with his heart racing. He woke the next day feeling lethargic and drained, not being able to recall anything from the night in detail, only vague feelings and impressions. He again worked through his chores and headed to his grandmother's house. As he walked through the door, he was greeted kindly by his waiting grandmother.

"Hello Japheth, you look about like I expected you to look," she said.

"I had another rough night, I'm not sure how sharp I will be today," he replied.

"Sit down, and I'll get you something that may help," she added.

Japheth sat down and watched as his grandmother walked to her open cupboard and pulled out a clear bottle that was filled with a yellowish liquid. She poured some out into a small porcelain cup. She then grabbed another bottle that had a white powder in it and put just a pinch into the cup. She handed it to Japheth and said, "Here, drink up, it will make you feel better."

He took the cup and sniffed it. It seemed to smell alright, in fact, it was a pleasing smell. With little thought, he quickly drank it down. He felt a slight twinge in his gut, and he immediately began to come out of his fatigue induced haze. "Thank you," he said.

"You're welcome."

"What is this?" he asked.

"It's probably better that you don't know," she said with a smile. "Are you ready to continue on with your studies?"

With an unsure look on his face, Japheth hesitated, then said, "I don't know if I can do it, there is too much on my mind from all of this, and I feel exhausted. I don't think I can handle anymore. However, I know I need you to teach me all that you can as quickly as you can, so I will to try."

Tabitha looked at him understandingly and said, "Japheth if you'll trust me and at least finish the book today I will give you something to help you get some rest this evening."

Japheth nodded his head and said, "Alright."

The book was again brought to Japheth and he began reading where he had left off. The remainder of the stories were as before, either extremely uplifting and confidence inspiring, or bleak and dismal. Once he was finished with the stories he moved back to the list of spells and began studying. As he read a question came to his mind, which he asked to his grandmother, "Where did these spells come from?"

She answered, "I can't tell you with any certainty, but the oral tradition is that the words came from an old, mostly forgotten language that has been lost to time. To my knowledge, the only remainders we have of it are the spells we use, although there are whisperings of an ancient book that contained the old language and was a type of translating tool for other languages. It was said that the book was taken to Ferox and deposited in a cave for safekeeping, but that story is centuries old. I doubt there is any truth to it."

Japheth's attention was peaked, "So if we could somehow learn that language, we could possibly have access to more spells, and it could help us to better use Lux also."

Tabitha replied, "Yes that is true, but it is only a legend. Even if it is accurate there hasn't been any person, wizards included, for centuries that have gone into Ferox and returned."

Ferox was well known in this part of the country. Its border began many days travel south of Licentia. It was a mountainous area with many different environments. There was everything from disease-ridden swamps, to arid deserts, volcanoes, and thick, dark forests. It had all types of feral animals that seemed to be extremely vicious, to the point of being rabid. There were also rumored to be many mythological creatures there with comparable temperaments.

Ferox seemed to have extreme weather also. Fierce winds, impenetrable rain, lightning storms, and lava flows were just some of the seemingly unnatural weather that the grounds experienced. It was also believed that the land itself was alive and would impede any explorer that may try to traverse the area. The land and the animals there seemed to have a symbiotic relationship, each protecting the other from outsiders. Rarely was there any news of someone trying to cross into Ferox, and when the effort was made, they were not heard from again.

Tabitha continued, "You have enough to learn right now without adding speculation like that into your thinking. Focus on what you have in front of you. Maybe one day, if it seems right, you could entertain the thought of finding that book and advancing our family's knowledge and understanding, but I think it best if you put it aside for now."

Japheth continued reading through the spells, focusing particularly on the ones that only worked with Lux. He noted again how much more powerful they were than the other spells. As night approached Tabitha began making another solution. Upon its completion she interrupted Japheth and bid him go home for the evening. "Japheth take this, go straight home, and get into your bed. You will sleep soundly and be well rested for tomorrow."

"I will, but I am still a little nervous about trying to sleep tonight," he said.

"Don't be, this will do the trick, it will be the best night sleep you've had in a while," she added. "I noticed you skipped over the potion section of the book, is there a reason for that?"

Japheth replied, "I am not too interested in potions, they seem like they might not be as important as some of the other material in the book."

"I know it may seem that way, but a properly made potion can be just what you need. It may not be intuitive, but they can be more beneficial than spells in the right situations. You would do well to learn them and commit them to memory, as you will the spells," she advised. "Now run on home and remember to get right into bed."

Japheth drank the concoction down and did as his grandmother had asked. He had barely gotten into bed when he felt his entire body relax and he was soon in a deep, restful sleep.

CHAPTER 5

Japheth's routine continued day after day, then week after week. He rose early, finished his chores, and went to his grandmothers. Tabitha was impressed at the amount of information he was able to absorb each day, and the more Japheth learned the more excited he became about his mother's family heritage of wizardry. He began memorizing the spells rapidly. He was still reluctant to study potions, but he did make some time for them each day, Tabitha saw to that. He also poured through the stories in the book over and over so that each lesson was documented in his memory.

His sleep had become somewhat restful, especially once he became more and more familiar with the stories. Once the initial shock of the stories was over, he could better cope with the uncomfortable tales in the book. He asked his grandmother for more of the potion that had helped him sleep, but she was disinclined to prepare it for him each night. She explained to him that although the potions she had given him could help him be alert, or help him rest, he must not become dependent on them or he would struggle to function normally when they were not available. As occasion called for, she would make another, but they were few and far between.

When Japheth showed up at his grandmother's house one mid-summer morning, he noticed that the book was not out as it had always been upon his arrival. Tabitha greeted him and said, "I think the knowledge you have gained needs to be supplemented with some practical application. Hence, part of your studies each day will be concocting potions and practicing spells that you have learned. I have also been wondering if you could use your bow or knives in conjunction with your spells."

Japheth asked, "What do you mean?"

"I think you might be able to shoot an arrow, or maybe throw a knife while casting a spell and have the spell adhere, for lack of a better term, to the arrow or knife, increasing the effectiveness and power of each."

Japheth smiled, liking the idea of meshing his old skills with the new knowledge he had gained. "I hope it works," he said.

They headed outside to begin practicing. As they ran through the list of spells that Japheth could remember, sometimes they worked and sometimes they didn't. Japheth was somewhat disappointed when his ignis spell was not the same as when he had used it on the wolves. There was a much smaller ball of fire that leaped from his hand, and it wasn't nearly as intense. He noticed that how loud he yelled did influence whether the spell worked or not. He asked his grandmother about the correlation. "If I yell louder it seems that the spell is more likely to work or maybe even be a little more powerful. Are those two things related?"

Tabitha responded, "Not really. Whether or not a spell works, and to what degree it works depends on the intensity of the one casting it. If you yell, that does help add more feeling and conviction, but you don't need to yell to get more out of a spell. My father always said that the mark of an exceptional wizard is that they could get the most out of a spell simply by whispering the words and letting the rest of the power come from them. It is something that you can only learn through practice. The ignis spell you used on the wolves is a good example. You were desperate. You and your father were in grave danger, and that affected the amount of fervency you put into the spell."

"Yes, but I also had Lux, that is the reason the spell was so powerful," Japheth replied.

Tabitha responded, "I'm sure that is a part of it, but I'm equally as sure that it's not all of it. Once you've practiced more you will understand, and hopefully, you will learn how to put more energy into your spells."

The rest of the day was spent on potion preparation with his aunt

Deborah. She was the apothecary of the family. Even though she did not have full-time access to the book, she had worked with her mother to memorize the details of each potion. They walked around the meadow, and along the edge of the forest looking for the ingredients for the potions they used. There were a good many important ingredients just a short distance into the forest, but no one had ventured into the forest in weeks, and they weren't inclined to start now.

Potions were also useful for healing, and as Japheth had experienced, lifting your spirits, or helping you to relax. Japheth balked at the idea of spending time on potion making, but his grandmother was insistent.

Deborah explained to Japheth, "Potions play an important role in our lives. Every known spell has a counter to it. Some spells are countered with other spells, but some spells are counteracted with potions. In general, the more powerful a potion is, the more dangerous it is to formulate. If you want to make potions that are powerful you must learn to prepare them exactly as you should."

The latter part of the day was spent grinding and mixing ingredients. A potion that they used extensively but were almost out of was crescere. It acted as a type of hyper fertilizer that would significantly shorten the growing time of their crops and garden vegetables. Deborah knew that it was very volatile if it was not mixed properly. She let Japheth do the mixing. He did not follow the instructions closely, and he ended up with a face full of ingredients.

"Now Japheth, I let you make that mistake on purpose," Deborah said with a smirk.

"Why would you do that?"

She responded, "The lessons you learn best and tend to remember longer, are the ones you learn by experience. I knew that if you were not meticulous in following the directions it would erupt. There is no harm in this happening with this potion, but there are many potions that if you are not careful you will end up severely maimed or possibly dead. I wanted this to happen to you so that you would remember to follow the instructions perfectly."

Japheth continued this pattern of study for another six weeks.

He had become much better at his spell casting and had also gotten a good start on potion making, becoming almost comfortable with it. Once he had gotten more proficient, he had spent a substantial amount of time trying to tie his spells together with an arrow as he shot it, or a knife as he threw it. For the most part, it was ineffective. When the two actions did coordinate it seemed to be more coincidence than anything else. Frustrated, Japheth was going to give up until one day Tabitha had an idea. "Japheth, I think we should try one more thing before we give up."

"What is that grandmother?"

"I have never heard of something like this having even been tried, so I don't know if will work, but I'd like to try," she answered. "I want you to throw a knife while at the same time using the ignis spell. When you do, I will use the spell to join or connect, apio, and we'll see if it will bind those two actions together. Apio is only used for physically binding things as far as I know, and I don't know of any situation where two wizards have used spells in conjunction with one another, so if this does work it would be a more important find than just binding a knife with fire."

Japheth seemed to understand the gravity of what they were trying and was excited by the prospect of success. "Alright grandmother, let's make spellcasting history!"

Japheth drew a throwing knife rom its sheath, looked at Tabitha, smiled, and said, "Ready?"

Tabitha nodded her head, and Japheth threw the knife while emphatically yelling, "Ignis!" At the same moment, Tabitha muttered, "Apio." The knife flew through the air towards the practice tree they had been using, with a small ball of fire just in front of it. The spheroid flew straight into the tree, which had long since died, while the knife was slightly off mark. It grazed the side of the tree and continued past. It was evident to both that their experiment had not worked. Japheth was visibly disappointed.

Tabitha looked at him and said, "Let's try a few more times before we give up. Something that is potentially this important shouldn't be given up on after one failure."

Japheth nodded his head in acceptance and threw another knife, with similar results. He had hit the tree this time, but the fire orb had hit the tree well before the knife. Again, Japheth's skepticism showed.

"One more time," Tabitha implored. Japheth grabbed for his last knife, reached back and threw again. Again, it had not worked.

"Well, that was amusing," Japheth said as he gathered his knives.

Tabitha asked quizzically, "Why don't you try both, use apio just prior to ignis and see what happens, the worst it will do is not work."

Once again, though skeptical, Japheth respectfully complied with his grandmother's request. He pulled a knife out, took a deep breath, and spoke both spells swiftly as he threw his knife. His concentration was divided between throwing his knife and getting both spells spoken quickly together. As a result, the knife missed the tree, but to the astonishment of both, the ball of fire followed the knife on its path through the air and past the tree instead of hitting the tree directly as before.

Japheth looked at Tabitha and said excitedly, "It worked!"

"Yes!" she responded, somewhat excited herself. "Now try it again."

Japheth was preparing to throw again when they heard the pounding of running horses' hooves on the road. It was two riders from Licentia. They hastily jumped from their mounts and rushed to talk to Tabitha.

"We need all of you to come to town quickly!" they pleaded.

"Why?" Tabitha asked.

"There is a group of men claiming to have an ultimatum. We believe it is coming from the king, but they refuse to say. They are dressed in his soldier's uniforms."

She asked again, "Did they say anything else?"

"No, they are just waiting at the inn. They say they won't talk until every prominent member of town is present."

Tabitha said, "We'll be there shortly. Japheth run and tell your parents to come."

Japheth and Tabitha gathered the family to Tabitha's house where the riders repeated their story. "There are men in town, we believe they were sent by the king. They say they have an important ultimatum for the town."

"How credible do you believe they are?" Eli asked.

"Very credible, one or all of them could be wizards, that's why we came for you," the riders answered.

The part of the answer that did not surprise the family was that they may be needed for their special abilities. The people in town did not associate much with them, and when they did it was usually out of necessity. The part about them being wizards was unexpected and made all the adults nervous. The family consulted with one another and resolved to leave Japheth with the rest of the adolescents and children while the adults went to town. Japheth adamantly objected but Eli explained to him that something seemed a bit off if they want all of the notable people in town gathered together. They also needed a capable person to stay with the rest of the family. Japheth reluctantly agreed.

Some of the older children that could use weapons were given the ones they were familiar with, just in case they needed them. Some also knew some spells, and each was briefly spoken to about what to do if the need should arise. They were all taken to the barn along with some bedding, and food in the event that they were there overnight. The doors were locked from the inside and Japheth found a place in the loft where he could see a good distance in each direction. They settled in to await the return of their family.

<hr />

The remainder of Japheth's family scaled their horses and began riding towards Licentia, accompanied by the riders from town. Eli grabbed his bow, throwing knives, and sword. Deborah brought a few potions that may be useful, and they started down the road.

On the way, they knew it was vital that they learn all they could before they arrived in town.

Tabitha asked, "Why do you think they might be wizards if they are dressed like the king's soldiers?"

The more assertive of the two riders raised an eyebrow and responded, "One of them lit a lantern in the inn with a small flame from his finger."

"That takes the guesswork out of it I suppose," she replied. "Do you know if they are all magical?"

"No, that's all we know for sure," the same rider said.

Tabitha continued, "Did they give any clue as to what their message is?"

"No. When they came into town they wanted to talk to the magistrate, when we told them we didn't have one they were a little confused. They asked who made the decisions for the community and we told them that each man governs himself. They counseled briefly and told us to gather all the important people in the community."

Tabitha and the riders alternated questions and answers for the bulk of the ride to Licentia, but the riders were not able to give any more telling information.

The group rode into town, hitched their horses, and proceeded to the location outside where everyone had gathered. Upon their arrival, one of the messengers inquired, "Are these the last that need to be here?" There was a general agreeance and nodding of heads among those gathered.

The messenger spoke in a loud, clear, confident voice. "People of Licentia listen well. We bring a message of peace and brotherhood. We are emissaries of Vesuvius, the most powerful wizard since the legendary Merlin. He desires peace with your community. His objective is grand and far-reaching, a unification of all mankind." Here the messenger paused to allow some contemplation. "Vesuvius desires the whole of the known world to be united as one, with him at the head to benevolently lead and guide humanity. There is no room for debate or compromise, only order and compliance.

"History has shown that men can never truly be at peace. Man's history is one of continual warfare, be it man against man, or kingdom versus kingdom. There has always been, and there always will be contention and bloodshed unless we are united under the same faction. A faction of harmony, one with another. A faction of justice and civility. A faction led and guided by a wise and ageless sage, with the ability and passion to bring it to pass. On my word, Vesuvius is that man. He is that wizard. Those who join with us will see paradise on this earth. For those that do not, only death awaits. What do you say people of Licentia?"

There was some mumbling from the crowd before an anonymous voice asked, "What about the king? What says he?" The question seemed to rouse the crowd some.

The messenger smiled slyly and continued, "We visited your king and presented much the same message. His arrogance would not allow him to see the opportunity laid at his feet. He denied our request, and now he and those with him sleep with their ancestors."

"I don't believe it," said another unclaimed voice, causing a low murmur to echo through the crowd.

The messenger went on, "So, my word is not good enough. Do we not wear the apparel of the king's soldiers? I recognize that a man can only believe what he sees, so believe this!" He outstretched his arm, as Tabitha noticed him mutter, and the oak tree next to the crowd began to freeze. The ice started at the base of the tree and gradually worked its way up the trunk and along the branches until the entire tree was enveloped. As he continued to hold his hand up and concentrate, the tree began to snap and crack, finally, there was an intense pop as the tree shattered into countless small pieces of ice.

The messenger waited for the uncomfortable silence to soften the tone of the crowd before speaking. "Just as that tree has been destroyed, so will you if you do not vow your loyalty to Vesuvius."

Silence cloaked the town, no one dared to speak. Eli could sense the growing tension and felt an altercation was imminent. He thought it best to try to work his way behind the messengers without being noticed. Tabitha, Abigail, and Adam, Deborah's husband, had worked their way to the front of the body, anticipating trouble as well.

The blacksmith, Aaron, a well-respected man in the town, began moving through the gathering until he stood in front of them, next to the messengers. Without acknowledging the foreign agents, he turned to address his friends and neighbors.

"My fellow Licentians, do not be charmed by this man's words. Have we not heard similar promises from different kings if we would align ourselves with them? They always promise unity, peace, and protection, but they are slow to explain the cost. These things cannot come about without subordination and a degree of slavery. We have always been a free people, free from rulers, free from bondage and oppression. We have been free to do as we choose while honoring the freedom of others. Let us keep to this custom, let us keep this privilege. It is better to pursue this course, come what may, than to live a life of servitude. That is the maxim we have lived by these many years, and it has served us well. This Vesuvius wishes us to abandon our freedom, I say let him come and try to take it!" After speaking, Aaron turned to face the messengers.

The emotions of the crowd began to stir in favor of the blacksmith's words. This visible and audible agreeance irked the head messenger.

"Fools!" he bellowed. "Silence you fools! You have no hope. Vesuvius can destroy your entire town with little effort. The display of my power is nothing compared to his. You will die if you do not conform. Again, I ask, and for the final time, what do you say? Do you wish to do as I say, and be part of bringing about utopia, or do you wish to follow this man down the road of certain death and destruction?"

There was silence from the crowd until one man called out, "I'll hitch my wagon to Aaron's."

A chorus of agreement followed from the crowd. The messenger looked to the ground and said calmly, "Very well." He made a backhand motion towards Aaron, which knocked him to the ground unconscious.

He stretched out his hand to his right and yelled, "Ignis!" As he did, not a ball, but a continuous stream of fire leapt from his hand. He moved his hand back across his body. As he did the greater part of the crowd began to flee. The flame quickly subsided and when the smoke thinned there stood Tabitha, with her own hand upraised, successfully countering his spell.

CHAPTER 6

"**W**itch!" the messenger roared. It had long been the custom in wizardry to refer to those that were not as skilled in magic as a witch or warlock. The title of wizard was reserved for only the most powerful individuals.

"I prefer to be called wizard," Tabitha replied.

The messenger returned, "I doubt you have reached the level of a true wizard, let us see."

By this time the crowd was in full retreat to their homes, or for some, into the forest. Tabitha stood directly in front of the four messengers. Abigail and Adam remained in their places as well, to either side of the messengers. Eli had worked his way around somewhat behind the messengers undetected. As the lead messenger spoke, the others grouped in tighter to him and one turned to face their rearward.

The messenger continued, "More than one witch I see. We shall make short work of you, and then see that this town is burned to the ground, with no one left to tell the story of your stupidity."

The wizard to the right of the group stomped his foot to the ground while peering at Adam. A small mound of dirt arose in front of him and quickly traveled towards Adam. When the mound was only a few feet in front of him it exploded into what looked like a small bolt of lightning and encompassed Adam. He fell to the ground moaning in pain.

The messenger in the back had let his attention drift to Adam, and Eli used this as his opportunity. He had already retrieved three arrows from his quiver, nocked one, and was ready to use them now. He spun around the corner of a house and fired three rapid shots at the distracted messenger. All three arrows found their mark, and he hit the ground dead.

Tabitha and Abigail had begun alternating spells back and forth with the remaining messengers. The barrage of spells created a thick mixture of steam, smoke, and dust. Each spell was seemingly countered as they volleyed back and forth.

The messenger that had attacked Adam noticed that the wizard in the rear had fallen and he speedily moved to take his place. As he turned, his attention fell on Eli, who was in the process of firing more arrows. The messenger held out his hand as the first arrow was fired. The arrow disintegrated midway in its flight, as did the one following. Eli darted back behind the house. The messenger shot a stream of fire from his hand that descended on the house that Eli used for cover. Eli knew he would be waiting for him to make a run for it, so he waited.

Abigail and Tabitha were still engaged with the two remaining messengers. Each interaction seemed to heighten the intensity of the battle, but neither pair was able to gain the upper hand. The cloud caused by the interactions of spells and counter spells continued to thicken. Deborah had drug Adam out of harm's way and was beginning to treat him for the burns he had received, his body involuntarily twitched as he struggled to stay conscious.

Eli had waited as long as he dared and was about to move when he saw a stranger climbing onto the roof of the house next to him. He waited a few moments more to see what he would do. As the stranger neared the peak of the roof, he removed a small throwing ax from his belt, looked directly at Eli and nodded his head. Eli nodded back in acknowledgment, not knowing exactly their course of action, but he understood he should ready himself. He nocked an arrow and watched the stranger. As the stranger stood and brought back the ax to throw, he let out a boisterous yell, announcing his presence in the fight. At the same instant, Eli skirted around the corner to aim at the messenger.

The stranger's yell grabbed the attention of the messenger who looked away from Eli's direction and focused on this new threat. As the ax hurtled towards him, the messenger reached out with his hand and the ax burst into numberless pieces of ice, as the oak tree had done only moments earlier. This gave Eli the instant he needed to fire off two arrows. The first one caught him in the shoulder, the second in the temple. Like his accomplice before him, he fell to the ground dead.

The messengers contending with Tabitha and Abigail did not notice their fallen friend because of the fierceness of the battle they faced in front of them. The two messengers were clearly more skilled at battle, but the mother-daughter duo could do enough to occupy them and wait for assistance.

Eli was reaching for more arrows when he saw movement out of the corner of his eye. The stranger had risen, thrown his ax, and taken cover behind the peak of the roof. Once Eli had fired, the stranger had risen again, drawn his sword, and was running down the pitch of the roof. Eli watched as the stranger leapt from the end of the roof, with his sword raised over his head with both hands. The stranger flew through the air towards the two remaining messengers. He brought his sword down just to the left of one's head, splitting him in two midway through his torso, as he crashed to the ground.

This startled the lone surviving messenger, the one that had taken the lead in delivering their message. It seemed to ignite a fury within him. Even though he was outnumbered and surrounded, he would not yield. He again made the backhanding gesture, and the stranger slid along the ground away from him in agony.

Eli shot two arrows which again disintegrated in their flight, seemingly without the messenger even seeing them. The stranger remained injured on the ground. Eli drew his sword and charged, yelling as he neared the battle. His yell was enough to distract the messenger for a brief moment. He reached a hand out towards Eli, and Tabitha saw her opportunity.

"Glacies!" she yelled.

The last remaining messenger was bombarded with small fragments of ice, each of which penetrated into the messenger's body, a few went completely through it. He fell back, stumbling on the bodies of his fallen companions. Eli, Tabitha, and Abigail cautiously approached him.

He lay on the ground coughing and sputtering. He looked up at the trio and half smiled. "You cannot win. Vesuvius will come, and there will be nothing left but scorched earth. His army will overwhelm you." He hacked and spit some more. "He will not even lose...a man. If you do somehow survive, he will simply send in his dragons, of which there is no escape. My only regret is that I won't be here to witness it. Just to give you a sporting chance, Vesuvius is expecting to meet us in two days. If we don't make it, he'll be here in three." The messengers head fell back, and he departed this life.

Tabitha, Abigail, and Eli hurried over to Adam and Deborah. Adam was still conscious, but in a great deal of pain. Deborah had put a potion on his skin to soothe the burns he had received and had also given him another to help dull the pain.

Tabitha said to Abigail, "I think he'll be alright, he's hurt, but he'll be alright."

They were interrupted by some of the townspeople that had approached them. "What can we do now? Do we stay and wait, or should we run?"

They went on with similar questions not addressed to anyone in particular.

Tabitha finally spoke up, "I think we need to get anyone that is outside of town, into town and then meet to discuss our options. Whatever we decide, we'll be better off if we stay together and stay united."

Abigail and Eli had moved to Aaron and the stranger to see if they were alright. Both were shaken up and hurting but not injured too badly. Abigail carefully helped Aaron to is feet and helped to dust him off. Eli extended his hand to the stranger and helped him rise.

Eli said, "Well stranger, we owe you many thanks, what is your name?"

"My name is Thaddeus," he replied.

Eli asked, "What has brought you to Licentia?"

"Vesuvius," was his answer.

Eli looked somewhat puzzled. "I don't understand."

Thaddeus responded, "I can tell you more, please just give me a few moments to recover."

"Of course," Eli said.

Thaddeus, Aaron, and Adam were taken to the inn to rest. Adam was put into a room with a bed to lie down in and be attended to. Thaddeus and Aaron sat at one of the tables. The townspeople began to gather around to find out more about this stranger.

Eli inquired, "How has Vesuvius brought you to Licentia?"

Thaddeus took a deep breath and began to tell his story.

"I was in the king's army when Vesuvius came, alone, to see the king. He gave an ultimatum to the king, much like I assume he gave to this town. When the king refused, he killed everyone in the castle. With the king and many nobles dead, things fell into disarray and the army scattered. I suppose that every man returned to his home.

"I had been home in Concederet for a few days when some messengers came and delivered the same message to my town. I spoke up and convinced them to agree to the messenger's terms. It was not difficult, as I had told them how easily Vesuvius had defeated the king's guards.

"Things returned to normal fairly quickly. We had been required to pay a higher tax than when we were under the rule of the king, but that seemed like an easy burden to bear. Then one day another messenger came and asked for young men to volunteer for Vesuvius' army. A few volunteered, mostly out of fear, and left with the messenger. A few days later the messenger returned, asking for more volunteers. When none could be found, he conscripted many, my son being one of them. This caused much uneasiness in our town, but we didn't dare cross him. He came back a third time with the same request and was met with open revolt.

"The messenger was killed, and then we waited to see the consequences of our actions. A few days later, just after breakfast, an army approached our town. We readied ourselves and met them in open battle. Vesuvius' soldiers were not as skilled as were we, but they were heavily armored, and they vastly outnumbered us. As the battle raged on it became horrid. Our women and children fled into the forest. As our forces broke down, they pursued us.

"I had determined to do all I could to defend my family. I continued fighting on into the forest. I had hidden myself behind a tree, and as a soldier approached, I ran him through. The resulting scream sounded hauntingly familiar."

At this point, Thaddeus paused as some mournful emotion had found its way into his words. He waited a few moments before continuing.

"I pulled the helmet off the bleeding soldier and stared into the eyes of my son. My heart sank and I was heartbroken. I knelt down and tried to comfort him, but he pushed me away. He cursed me and sputtered like he had no idea I was his father, as he tried not to die. His strength soon failed him, and he could not stop me from holding him as I sobbed. Shortly thereafter he passed away in my arms."

An eerie silence had fallen over the entire inn. Not a sound was made in the entire building.

"I was filled with rage and hate, but not at the soldiers that were attacking us. I knew many of them were our own sons. My hate was aimed at Vesuvius.

"I got up and ran. I tried to follow the sounds of battle, but I was unable to find the source of it through the trees. It was an awful sound. From the cries I heard, I believe the soldiers had started to find our women and children hiding in the forest, for which there was no mercy.

"I tripped as I was making my way down a slope and hit my head. I awoke the next day to silence. I backtracked my way to town only to find it had been burnt to the ground. Looking back, I think it must have been his dragons, no man-made fire could cause that type of destruction. There were no clues that there had been structures of any kind. It was nothing but ash-covered earth.

"I don't know what Vesuvius did to the minds of our sons to make them kill their own so readily, but I vowed not to rest until I have my revenge, or I find the peace that can only come with death.

"I have spent all of my time from that day trying to find Vesuvius. I followed his messengers here, and now that they are dead, he will surely come, and I will have my opportunity for revenge."

The entire inn remained silent as the horror of Thaddeus' words sank in, each believing it was a foreshadowing of the fate of Licentia.

CHAPTER 7

Japheth had seen the smoke and dust that had risen from the fight in Licentia. His first impulse was to rush to help, but wanting to honor the request of his parents, he stayed put to look after his younger family members. After the air had cleared, he could see his father coming down the road towards their home. He unbarred the barn door and rushed to meet him, the younger children following closely behind.

Japheth excitedly asked, "What happened?"

Eli responded, "I can tell you as we gather our things." He looked over the group and announced, "I need all of your help. We are collecting what things we will need for a few days and heading to Licentia."

Each child was given instructions on what to get and put into the wagon. Japheth remained close to his father so that he might hear of what went on. As the pair worked on loading the bigger items, Eli told the entire story of what had happened to Japheth. He left out part of Thaddeus' story so as not to upset any listening ears that may have been eavesdropping.

Many of the children had questions which they fired off rapidly at Eli as they rode into Licentia. He answered them honestly and bluntly. Most of their questions had been answered as the group reached town. There were some other people from outlying areas that were arriving at the same time, and more where still expected.

Eli and Japheth joined the people of Licentia, who were holding a meeting inside the church to discuss their next course of action. The consensus was that something terrible, most likely an army, was coming, but what they should do about it was still open for debate. Thaddeus' story had been spread throughout the town, and every person knew what type of enemy they faced.

Tabitha believed they should run, and she said as much. "If those wizards are not as powerful as Vesuvius, we won't have a chance. Even if we can defeat his army of men, I doubt we can be victorious against him, especially if he has dragons at his command."

Aaron, who was in favor of standing their ground, took his turn to speak. "What about your sword Tabitha? Doesn't it have enough power to defeat Vesuvius?"

"Yes, I suppose in the right hands it does, but I no longer have it."

There was some murmuring from the crowd before someone asked, "Where is it?"

It was a question Tabitha didn't want to answer. Japheth had been a tremendous student but was not ready for a task of this magnitude.

"It's been given to my grandson Japheth," she replied.

"Why does that boy have it?" came another question from the crowd.

Tabitha answered, "Because it is time for it to be passed on. Japheth has been an excellent pupil, but he does not have the knowledge, or experience to defeat someone as powerful as I believe Vesuvius is. I believe he has gained power over the animals, and that is what has made them act so strangely for so long.

"Those messengers were more powerful than almost any of the wizards that we have record of, and much more so than any currently in our family. We were able to defeat them because we had the element of surprise on our side and assistance from Thaddeus. Without those advantages, I fear the outcome may have been much different."

A faceless voice from the crowd requested, "Take the sword for now, and give it back when this ordeal is over."

"That is not how it works. I can no longer use the sword in that manner, only Japheth can."

There was some more murmuring from the crowd when

someone asked, "What does Thaddeus suggest? He has seen Vesuvius' workings up close."

The crowd quieted as Thaddeus arose and spoke. "While I have been following Vesuvius, I have seen some towns capitulate, some fight, and some flee. The only difference in outcome is those that subject themselves to his rule survive, but ultimately are little more than slaves. The rest are utterly destroyed. I believe you have lost the option of being his subjects. The only question left is, do you want to die facing your enemy, or running from him? I regret the counsel I gave to my own town. If I had to choose again, I would have chosen to die fighting alongside my son instead of against him. Regardless of what you choose, I am staying here to wait for Vesuvius."

The crowd continued to debate, but whatever momentum Tabitha may have created to persuade the people to flee was squelched by Thaddeus' words. There were a few families that still desired to run. They were allowed to leave but not ensured of any help as the whole of the town would be occupied in preparing for Vesuvius' visit.

Tabitha spoke. "Lux has the power to blind. If Vesuvius does control the animals in the forest, we could use that to render them helpless, it could also work if he chooses to attack with an army of men."

A skeptical individual spoke up, "What if it blinds us as well?"

Tabitha answered, "We will put the counter spell on each person in town so that you will not be affected by the blinding power of Lux."

There was a general agreement and the discussion moved on with Tabitha still having the floor. "We will place Japheth on the bell tower in the center of town. When he is alerted of the approaching threat, he will use Lux to blind them."

"What if it doesn't work?" came another question from the group.

Eli's powerful voice answered the question, "Then we fight."

Tabitha agreed. "Yes, we fight. Japheth will do all he can from the bell tower. Once we are engaged with them, he will need to come down and join us. From his vantage point, he can see where he would be most needed."

Eli interrupted, "We need to place lookouts at the tree line to give us some advance warning."

"Agreed," said Tabitha. "They should be given a bell of some sort to ring as an alarm once the approaching threat is sighted."

The body continued discussing their preparation plans. It was decided to try to construct a wall around Licentia. The houses along the outside of town would be used as part of the wall. The spaces in between would be built up with timbers to form a wall. One end would be sharpened to a point and the other end would be buried in the ground with all poles lashed together.

Once the plans were put into place another question was asked, "What if he has dragons?"

Silence filled the church until Deborah responded. "There is always dragonsbane. If what we believe about dragons is true, they will be nearly impossible to defeat. If Vesuvius does have dragons it is something that we must have. Anyone other than Japheth has virtually no chance without it."

Tabitha was hesitant. "I'm afraid having it may be too dangerous, I don't know how we could safely carry it."

"What is dragonsbane?" Aaron asked.

Deborah explained, "It is a scarce plant. I don't believe it is natural. Legend states it was created by wizards centuries ago. While it is green, it is harmless. When it is picked, dried, and ground the resulting powder is extremely incendiary. Once it's on your skin it will burn you, no matter how quickly you remove it, or wash it off. If it is inhaled or ingested, you will burn from the inside out. Dragon's skin is impervious to dragonsbane. It could be worth the risk, because if a dragon's skin is pierced with a weapon that has dragonsbane on it the dragon will completely lose its mind trying to stop the burning. I believe this is preferable to having them under Vesuvius' control."

Tabitha interjected, "It is much too dangerous to make." She turned to look at Deborah. "At the very least you will be burned from preparing it, and at worst you would endure an excruciating death."

"I think we should make some," said an anonymous voice from the crowd.

Tabitha turned and faced the crowd. "We don't even know if he has dragons. It is not worth the risk, but if someone would like to volunteer to harvest and make it please come forward."

Complete stillness filled the church, no one wanted to be mistaken for a volunteer.

"That's what I thought," she said. "Let's start our preparations for Vesuvius' visit."

Every able-bodied person was given a task. Many timbers needed to be cut and set into place. Numberless arrows needed to be made, and buildings fortified. On top of that, there were all the visitors that had moved in from outside of town that needed places to stay. It took total cooperation from everyone, but by the third day, their town was as fortified as it possibly could have been.

Japheth awoke early. He strapped Lux to his side and went outside. He was greeted by his grandmother. "Good morning Japheth."

"Good morning grandmother," he replied. "Do you think today is the day?"

"I do," she answered. "There is something different in the air. It seems as though all of nature is uneasy. The forest is unusually quiet. Vesuvius will be here today."

Japheth went on, "I'm nervous."

"As well you should be," she replied. "It is not an easy thing that is being asked of you, but I believe you are equal to the task. If you can recall what you have studied, you could very well protect and save us all."

"That's a lot of pressure," Japheth said.

"It is," she returned, "but it is your burden to bear. These are the moments when heroes are made."

Japheth half smiled and blushed. "I'm no hero grandmother."

"I think your father would say differently," she said. "As I have pondered on the stories from the book, I believe no matter what else happens today you will survive, but I'm just not sure about the rest of us."

Japheth asked, "Why do you say that?"

"That just seems to be the pattern of the one who wields Lux," she answered.

The rest of the townspeople were stirring and preparing for what they assumed would be coming that day. All the adults in Licentia, save for the lookouts at the forests edge, met one final time to revisit their plans.

Eli took charge. "The walls in between the houses have been constructed so that there are only two access points into town. Each point has been assigned two wizards and an equal number of archers. As discussed, the wizards and archers are to be out in front of the access points as the army approaches, to do as much damage as possible from a distance, before retreating inside.

"Once inside the archers are to climb on the rooftops while the wizards will be set at the access point. Once the intruders near the town, the wizards will use a spell to block the access point, not allowing them into town, for as long as possible so the archers will have more time to shoot down the enemy. Every house top has been stocked with bundles of arrows, running out should not be a concern.

"When they realize they cannot enter through the access point they will begin to move along the wall to find a place to climb over. We have constructed footbridges from roof to roof. The archers need to follow the enemy as they move along the outside of the wall and take down as many as they can.

"Once they are in, and they will get in, the archers are to stay focused on those outside of the wall. This will limit the number that get inside. Our soldiers are stationed equally throughout the border of the wall. Once the enemy enters, fight for your families and your freedom, I believe there will be no mercy for us. The women and children will be barricaded inside of the houses in the middle of town. They have been given weapons to defend themselves if it comes to that, but I pray it doesn't reach that point. Are there any questions?"

There was a grim silence from those gathered.

Aaron moved to the front of the crowd and spoke. "My fellow Licentians, let us fight bravely and valiantly. Our enemy desires our lives because we would not trade our freedom for servitude. Let him see how Licentians fight to maintain their freedom. If we should perish, we ultimately have the final victory, for no matter how powerful this Vesuvius is, he does not have it within his power to enslave us."

Aaron's words had an inspiring effect on the crowd, and it lifted their spirits as much as they could be.

Eli continued, "Everyone move to your assigned stations and prepare for what will most likely be most trying day of your lives."

The Licentians began moving to their places. Eli turned to speak with Japheth. "Son, since the day you saved me from the wolves, I have been impressed with the man you have become. I do not know what this day holds for us, but no matter how much you've read from that book, nothing can prepare you for the horrors of war. Keep your wits about you and you shall fare better than the rest of us. Fight bravely, and if there's no other choice, die with honor and courage."

Japheth wrapped his arms around his father in a rare hug.

"Thank you father, I love you."

"I love you too son."

Abigail moved in to embrace them both. After a few moments, the hug broke and Eli spoke again, "Let's get to our places."

Thaddeus approached the trio. "Eli, I would like to stay with Japheth. I'll admit it is for selfish reasons. I think if anyone gets close to Vesuvius it will be him. I give you my word that I will protect him with my life."

"Thank you," Eli said. "I would appreciate that."

The family moved along with everyone else in town until they were all in position and waiting. Japheth and Thaddeus climbed to the top of the bell tower and waited in silence.

Thaddeus spoke first. "Do you think you are ready?"

"No," was Japheth's honest reply. "I can't be as brave as you and my father. I heard how you fought against the messengers. I'm afraid I don't have that in me."

Thaddeus smiled and replied, "After hearing how you saved your father from the wolves, I will have to disagree with you. You are already every bit the hero your father and I are."

Japheth smiled. "Thank you."

As the conversation ended the ringing of a bell could be heard to the north of town. It rang furiously for a few short moments and then stopped immediately. The final ring echoed for an instant, and then there was complete silence as a single man walked out of the forest and moved towards Licentia.

CHAPTER 8

The lone figure continued walking towards Licentia. As he neared, he held his hands outstretched to the side in a non-threatening posture. Once he was within range he stopped and raised his deep, scratchy voice and called out to the people of Licentia.

"I come in peace. I mean you no harm. I have lost contact with four of my friends, and I desire to know concerning them."

There was silence and indecision from the Licentians. After a long, uncomfortable pause Aaron addressed the stranger. "What is your name?"

"My name is Vesuvius," he replied. A wave of panic swept over all within the sound of his voice.

Aaron responded, "Your friends are dead. They attacked our town unprovoked, and we defended ourselves as every man should. You are not welcome here, move along."

Vesuvius let this information soak in for a few moments and then responded, "My friends carried a message for me. A message of hope and order for mankind. Please allow me to approach so that I may better explain myself."

Tabitha looked at Aaron and shook her head. The sentiment was shared by all.

Aaron answered, "We are not interested in your proposal, we will not succumb to a ruler. We are free men and desire to stay as such, now move along."

Vesuvius began walking towards town again. As he moved closer the archers prepared themselves to fire. Tabitha and Abigail were stationed at the front of the crowd, and they readied themselves.

Aaron shouted out a warning, "Stop or our archers will fire upon you."

Vesuvius kept advancing on Licentia and Eli roared, "Fire!" The archers stationed on the rooftops let their arrows fly, and over a dozen barreled towards him. He never flinched as he continued to progress towards town. As the arrows neared him, they would simply burn up in an instant, leaving only a thin wisp of smoke.

Eli again yelled, "Fire!" The second round of arrows ended up like the first, as Vesuvius advanced. Once he was too close for Tabitha's liking she reached out a hand and yelled, "Inpulsa!" A small charge left her hand towards Vesuvius. As it neared him it fizzled out. He stopped and smiled.

"That's what I was looking for," he said. "A clue as to how you were able to defeat my men. I never considered that you would have wizards among you. What is your name?"

"Tabitha, descendant of Merlin."

He responded, "I take it you have a family history to show that."

"I do."

He continued, "In my studies, I have come across...shadows of information about a family relic that may have been Merlin's. Are any of those whisperings true?"

"If you are referencing his enchanted sword, yes they are true," she answered.

"And what of its limitless power, is that true as well?"

Tabitha responded, "It's power is not limitless, there is no such thing."

"Ah, but you underestimate what one can do with time, ambition, and patience. I believe anything that can be imagined can be brought to pass. Do you have this sword in your possession?" he asked.

"I do not," she replied.

"Alas, I should not be so fortunate to find such an item, but at least I have no need to fear you."

He looked at Aaron. "You seem to be the authority here, what is your name?"

"Aaron, and I am no authority. I am a blacksmith, each man here rules himself."

"Interesting," Vesuvius said as he smiled. He looked up and addressed everyone gathered.

"Those were some of the best men I had at my command. As I have moved forward with my plans to unify mankind, I have met much resistance, but I have never met successful resistance. That is why I have come, I want to alter my proposal for your town.

"The message my men brought was one of order, in place of the disorder that plagues mankind. It was a message of hope for the poor, and freedom for the downtrodden. Admittedly this cannot happen without some level of obedience to a benevolent architect.

"I know it was no small task to defeat my men, that is why I have personally come to offer you a better proposition. In the kingdom I am creating there will certainly be a need for a new class of nobles, those that I can rely on to oversee the affairs of the kingdom. You, people of Licentia, fit that mold. I need leaders to be strong, brave, and wise, which you must be if you've bettered my men.

"In my hundred and fifty years on this earth, I have seen what men do if left to themselves. I have also seen what a tyrant with power can do. I wish none of this to come to pass. There can be a glorious compromise that you can be part of. If you follow me you will never want for the necessities of life, and rarely will you want for the comforts. I can personally see that promise fulfilled to you, your children, and your grandchildren. I ask you, brave citizens of Licentia, will you be at the head of this beautiful future, or simply a stumbling block to my inevitable success?"

"We want no part of your future," Aaron responded. "No man has the right to rule over another, not in any degree."

Vesuvius replied, "While it may be true that no man has the right to rule over another, many have the ability. I thought each man here governed himself and should, therefore, answer for himself."

A lone voice bellowed out, "Here, here!" This lone answer was followed by a loud chorus of agreement from the people of Licentia.

"Pity," Vesuvius replied, "I hate to see individuals such as yourselves embrace their demise."

With that he began walking backward, always keeping an eye on the people until he disappeared back into the forest.

The town had waited for some time before they heard a bell from the east watchman begin to ring. Shortly thereafter the other two watchmen began ringing their bells. After ringing for a few minutes nothing could be seen by the townspeople. Then suddenly the ringing ceased. Still, the people waited but could not see anything emerging from the forest. The minutes passed like hours, everyone was anxious to know what had caused the bells to ring, and then stop.

Eventually, there was sound from the surrounding forest. It began as a slight rustling and got progressively louder. Then it seemed all at once the forest exploded with wolves. From every direction they poured out of the trees towards Licentia.

Japheth was alarmed and began to draw Lux from his scabbard. Thaddeus stopped him. "Not yet Japheth, make sure they have all left the safety of the forest so that you can blind them all."

Japheth nodded as he finished drawing Lux. As he did the rustling sound grew even louder and bears joined the charging wolves coming out of the forest. Japheth gauged that he could only wait for a few more moments. He raised Lux and prepared to utter his spell.

When he could wait no longer, he said, "Caecus." A bright surge of light exited Lux and traveled out in every direction. As the light came into contact with the charging animals the scene of carnage was terrible. Blinded by the spell, the animals stumbled into one another and began attacking each other mercilessly. They clawed, slashed, and bit at anything else they could sense.

Japheth watched from the bell tower, both intrigued and disturbed by what he witnessed. He could see that as an animal got too close to the town wall it was either shot by an archer or destroyed by a wizard. He could also faintly make out some small black somethings among the chaos. He saw a few of the bears and wolves that were not killed clumsily and blindly try to retreat back into the forest. When the turmoil had died down, he and Thaddeus climbed down from the tower to discover what had happened.

Japheth pushed through the crowd until he found Eli. "What happened?"

Eli replied, "Vesuvius came to offer us positions of power and authority in his new kingdom if we would join him."

Thaddeus interrupted, "That was Vesuvius?"

"Yes," Eli responded.

Thaddeus continued in disappointment, "Then I missed my chance. I didn't think he would come alone."

"I doubt he has come alone," Eli said.

As Eli finished, a man came running up to him. "The watchmen are all dead," the man said.

"How?" Eli inquired.

"The man to the north appears to have been crushed, but by what we can't tell."

"And what of the others?" Eli asked.

"Snake bites," he replied. "Probably the same ones that were attacking with the wolves and bears."

"Snakes?" Japheth asked.

"Yes," Eli replied. "We couldn't even see them in the grass until you blinded the animals. They must have started getting stepped on and then they turned on the wolves and bears. They aren't like any snakes I have seen. They are completely black and extremely venomous."

"I have seen snakes like those before," Thaddeus said. "When I was in the king's army, we were marching around Ferox and we ran into a few of them. They were highly aggressive. If a man was bitten, he was dead within minutes."

Eli turned to Japheth, "You had better get back up onto the bell tower, I doubt that is all we will see of Vesuvius this day. Just do the same as you have already done. If they have figured how to counter the spell, move down to the wall as we discussed."

With that Japheth and Thaddeus moved back to their places in the bell tower to wait.

Thaddeus was obviously disheartened at missing his chance to face Vesuvius.

Japheth spoke, trying to lift his spirits. "Thaddeus, I think you will yet have your chance at him. Once we defeat whatever type of army he has, surely he will come himself. He doesn't seem to be afraid of facing the entire town, he has already shown himself once."

"Perhaps you are right," Thaddeus replied. "For your towns sake, I hope you are not."

Japheth got a sick feeling in the pit of his stomach as Thaddeus' words sank in. It was then that Japheth realized that Thaddeus had no intention of living through his encounter with Vesuvius, nor did he think the town would.

There was silence in the bell tower for the remainder of their stay.

A few hours before dusk a bell began ringing and one of the lookouts was hurrying towards town. When he got in audible range he stopped, cupped his hands around his mouth, and yelled his warning, "Army!"

On his word, the archers and wizards moved outside of the wall and positioned themselves to attack. The sight of the approaching army was unnerving to the people of Licentia. Like in Thaddeus' story, they were well armored, well-armed, and large in number.

Japheth readied Lux again. He held the sword over his head and yelled, "Caecus!" Again, a wave of light traveled out from Lux. As it came into contact with the approaching army there was no noticeable disruption, it had not worked.

Thaddeus looked at Japheth and said, "You must go down, the spell has not worked. I will stay here, if there is some sort of trickery and you are needed near the other opening, I will ring the bell."

Japheth nodded and quickly made his way down the tower and towards the hole in the wall closest to the approaching army. As he neared, he could see the archers out front trying to stop them from a distance, but with little effect. Each soldier was equipped with armor covering his torso, head, and portions of their arms and legs. They had large, well-made shields and swords as well. As the archers fired into the oncoming men very few of them fell. As they came under fire, they quickened their pace towards the town. Once they closed in further, they were within the wizard's range.

Abigail and Tabitha unleashed their spells as quickly and powerfully as they could. There had been a few moments available for them to discuss how to best proceed, and they had decided that ignis would be the most effective against the heavily armored soldiers.

As the balls of fire hurtled towards the approaching soldiers, they made no attempt to avoid the spells, rather they ran directly into them. When the fire collided with a soldier, they were engulfed in flames but continued running towards the fortified town.

Japheth situated himself between his mother and grandmother. He could see that the ignis spell was not having the desired effect. He held Lux straight out in front of him and spoke. "Glacies." A thick cloud of large, jaggedly shaped ice crystals emanated from Lux and sped towards the rushing soldiers. The force of the spell knocked the men in front off their feet, while simultaneously extinguishing the fire that consumed them. The airborne ice had also found its way into every portion of the soldiers that was not covered by armor, killing many of them, and wounding all those in the lead.

He then turned to Abigail's side and repeated the spell. The rushing army had observed what had happened to their cohorts, and as he cast the spell, they raised their shields to block. The ice crystals slammed into the front line once again, but without the desired effect. They were able to brace themselves for the impact, and it only slowed them.

Japheth's mind raced for another spell. Inpulsa came to the front of his mind, and he uttered the spell. A bolt of what looked like lightning sprang out of Lux and swallowed up the invaders. The front two to three rows of attackers fell to the ground dead and smoldering. The immediate fall of those in front caused the remaining soldiers to stumble over their fallen comrades, greatly slowing their charge.

Japheth turned to Tabitha's side and repeated the spell, with similar, successful results.

At this point, because of the closeness of the attacking army, the archers had begun to move back inside of the wall and take their places on the housetops. Once the advancing men were closer to the wall Japheth felt confident that the archers could be more successful against the army. If they took careful aim, they could hit the areas that were not protected by armor.

Japheth watched as his mother and grandmother repeated the spell. Their efforts were not nearly as effective without the magnifying power of Lux, but they were able to somewhat stifle the army's advance.

He had just turned his attention to the foes in front of him when he heard a noise that dropped his heart into his stomach, the church bell. He knew that Thaddeus could see what was happening at both entrance points of the wall and that the circumstances at the other side must be dire if he rang the bell.

Japheth wagered that the ignis spell he could muster with Lux would have more of an effect than that of his mother and grandmother. He pointed Lux at the approaching army and yelled, "Ignis!"

A steady flow of fire came from the sword. It was not unexpected as Tabitha had told him about the messenger's spell doing the same. He swept his sword quickly from left to right across the attacking men.

As the flame bombarded the soldiers it proved significantly more powerful than the ones Abigail and Tabitha had cast. It caused the soldiers in front to collapse in burning heaps and become flaming stumbling blocks to those behind them.

Feeling that things on this end were more secure than before, he motioned for Abigail and Tabitha to get inside the wall. Even with the success of the spells, they would soon be overwhelmed because of the number of undaunted attackers that continued towards them. He turned to see the entrance in the wall full with retreating archers. He hoped his mother and grandmother could get inside before they were inundated.

Japheth knew he could not wait to get through the wall and then to the other side of the town in time to help, so he resolved to run around the outside of the wall. As this thought came into his mind he began to tingle, just as he had the day he had saved his father from the wolves. He smiled as everyone and everything around him seemed to slow down, except for himself.

CHAPTER 9

Tabitha and Abigail moved towards the entrance in the wall. The last of the archers were still waiting to file through the hole. The pair of wizards continued to assail the soldiers as they backed towards their place of retreat.

Tabitha glanced at Abigail and said, "You get through the opening first, and I'll follow. Then be prepared to cast your clipeum spell to keep them out."

"Okay," Abigail replied. "Say when."

As the advancing men grew closer Tabitha exclaimed, "Now!"

Abigail turned and darted through the hole in the wall, as she did Tabitha yelled, "Clipeum!" A large, nearly invisible disk formed in front of her outstretched hand. The charging men in the lead slammed into it at full running speed and were driven back as if they had run headlong into a stone wall. This caused the men behind to slam into the back of them, and into the disk again. Tabitha retracted her hand, causing the spell to break. The first few rows of men then stumbled forward over one another and onto the ground.

Tabitha scurried through the opening and Abigail stepped forward to cast her clipeum spell.

The rushing soldiers had trampled over those that had fallen and again slammed into the faintly visible disk, stopping them in their tracks. As the men began to pile up against the fortification, they started moving along the wall looking for another place to enter or climb the wall.

The intruders had now moved much closer to the archers, and as a result, they were able to have more of an effect because they could hit the areas that weren't protected by armor. More of their enemies began to fall, but the sheer number of attackers was disheartening to those in position to see the coming onslaught. As planned, some of the archers followed the soldiers as they spread around the wall.

After getting through the opening Tabitha hurried up the ladder to the rooftops, while Abigail continued to blockade the opening in the wall. As she stood with her hand outstretched, she could see the contorted, rage-filled faces of the soldiers that were still pressed up against her spell. It startled her to see such malevolence from an individual, and for the first time since the attack had begun, she felt the magnitude of the evil they faced.

She decided to try to cast the inpulsa spell through her clipeum spell. As she uttered the words a small shock left her unused hand and passed unimpeded through the nearly transparent shield. It struck a soldier and he fell to the ground. It was not as powerful as usual because she was casting two spells simultaneously. She continued to use the inpulsa spell while blocking the entrance in the wall. After seeing the danger they faced up close she knew they all must do everything they could if they were going to be victorious.

Tabitha made her way to the rooftop. She could see the charging enemy advancing towards their town. She wished for a moment that she still had Lux to magnify her powers. She quickly put the thought aside, knowing that it would not do any good. She began using the inpulsa spell as before with similar successful results.

Eli was atop the house opposite of Tabitha. Next to him was a barrel full of arrows. He would grab three to five at a time and fire them all in quick succession. Most of his arrows found their mark. Between him and Tabitha, they were keeping the rushing soldiers somewhat in check but they both noticed that, despite the great number of them falling, they continued spreading along the wall. Each time he reached for more arrows he would look to Abigail to see if she was tiring. After the battle had been raging for quite some time, he could see fatigue setting in.

Eli looked at Tabitha as he nodded his head towards Abigail. "Tabitha, she's tired!" he yelled.

Tabitha looked down at her daughter and nodded at Eli. She hurried down the ladder and took Abigail's place at the wall. After she was relieved, Abigail made her way to the ladder and tried to climb, but she collapsed to the ground exhausted. Eli took notice, but did not leave his post, he simply continued firing arrows.

From his vantage point, Eli could see some of the soldiers getting over the wall, but not nearly as many as he had anticipated. Much to his relief, he did not see any of the enemy making their way through the streets or between the houses. From the sounds of battle reaching his ears, he deduced that the ones that were making it over the wall were being handled by their armed soldiers within Licentia.

He also noticed that the number of advancing enemies was not innumerable, as he saw the last of them progressing towards town. He looked upon Tabitha who was keeping the opening in the wall closed off to the enemy. She was also becoming weary. The number of dead soldiers on the outside of the wall had become so numerous that it was an impediment to those still advancing.

He knew if he did not go down and assist Tabitha that she would soon be drained and collapse as Abigail had. He lowered the barrel of arrows down from the roof and then jumped to the ground. He hurried to Tabitha dragging the barrel and spoke. "Let's get Abigail and retreat deeper into town."

"I can't," she replied. "If I leave, they will gain entrance into the town."

"If you do not leave you will be exhausted, and they will gain entrance anyway, but you will be unable to retreat or defend yourself," Eli said as he looked back at Abigail, who had regained some of her strength. "Get Abigail and get back in behind some of our soldiers and get rested. I will hold this point in the wall."

Tabitha glanced at him curiously. "Not with magic, with this," he said as he held out his bow.

"Besides, I have seen the end of their forces, we may be able to hold them off."

"Very well," Tabitha said as she retracted her hand, breaking the spell that was blocking the entrance in the wall. She stumbled back slightly, but Abigail was there to catch her.

"Let's go, mother," She said as the drained pair began retreating away from the wall.

Eli had already clutched a fist full of arrows and had readied himself. Just a few moments after the spell was broken, he began firing. He fired at an incredibly rapid rate, and nearly every arrow found its mark. The soldiers were stumbling over the fallen and could not rush the entrance. Their slow advance left them as sitting ducks to his arrows.

Even though Eli was extremely fast and accurate he could not completely keep up with the number of assailants.

"Assistance!" he yelled to the archers on the houses on either side of him. One joined Eli to assure that the enemy was not able to enter through the opening in the wall. With the added help they were able to hold the enemy at bay, until Eli ran out of arrows.

As he fired his last arrow, Eli set his bow in the empty barrel, drew his sword and motioned for the waiting forces inside the wall to join him near the opening.

"Forward men of Licentia, steel thyselves and prepare to defend your freedom and families. I have seen the end of their army. If we fight bravely now, we can be victorious." Without hesitation, the men responded by moving forward and formed a living wall between the invading army and the heart of their town.

As the enemy soldiers climbed over their fallen peers they began to charge through the opening. They ran swiftly into the wall of waiting men. They swung their weapons wildly as they encountered the Licentians. It was soon apparent to Eli and those men that had been trained in combat, that these assailants had little to no training.

As more of them poured through the wall, the battle became grievous. The men of Licentia were much more skilled in battle, but because of the full body armor of the attackers it was difficult to cut them down. Slowly the armored soldiers began to overpower the Licentians simply because of their superior numbers.

When the first Licentians fell, they were quickly replaced by the man behind them. As they fell more frequently fear began to set in among them, and some men began to lose heart and flee from the enemy before them.

Eli noticed the fleeing individuals. Quickly he looked for an opportunity to get on top of a house so that he might address those engaged in battle, and those fleeing from it.

He saw an enemy soldier that had fallen and was kneeling on all fours. He sheathed his sword and ran towards him. As he reached him, he stepped onto his back and leapt for the roof. He landed with his arms on the roof, and quickly he pulled himself up and began addressing those in battle.

"Brothers of Licentia," his loud voice boomed as he held his hands in the air. "Do not flee, do not lose courage. Dig in, stand fast, and hold your ground, for your families and your freedom are depending on you!" His small bit of encouragement was enough to spur the retreating men back into battle.

With the invading forces quickly dwindling the Licentians were able to handle the remaining forces, and soon they stood with no one left to fight.

The men began to cheer, but were cut short by Eli, who motioning for a portion them to follow him, yelled, "To the other entrance!" He instructed the remaining men to stay there to guard the opening in the wall.

<hr>

Japheth sped around the outside of the wall towards the south end of town. His mind was racing through the possibilities that awaited him there. As he came around the side of the wall, he saw what appeared to be an infinite number of men rushing the town. These men were not armored at all, but they sprinted towards town as if possessed by an unseen force.

As planned the archers had moved out front and began firing

from a distance at the rapidly approaching army, with Debora and Adam assisting as they could. The archers had not yet filed inside the protective wall, which left Debora and Adam outside.

Japheth could see they would not all get inside before they were overtaken by the enemy. He also judged that at his pace he may be able to put himself between his aunt and uncle and certain death from the attackers.

His mind raced for an answer to what he should do. Just as he skidded to a stop in front of the retreating townspeople, he had an idea.

Holding Lux in one hand he crossed both arms in front of him and cast the ignis spell while uncrossing his arms. A river of fire was expelled from Lux and his off hand. As it came into contact with the approaching soldiers they fell almost instantly to the ground. The devastation did not slow the rest of the forces as they simply ran over the fallen, some catching fire themselves.

By now most of the archers had gotten to the rooftops and were firing at the invaders. Not being protected by armor, they began to fall by the dozens as they were fired upon. Still, it seemed as though an unending wave of soldiers continued to crash towards Licentia.

The first line of soldiers, most of them on fire, began to reach the wall and attempted to climb over. They were easily stopped by the archer's arrows. As they fell to the ground their burning bodies lay at the base of the wall and it began to catch fire.

Japheth got behind the safety of the wall as his aunt Debora blocked the entrance with her spell. He made his way to a rooftop to survey the situation. He looked out on the enemy forces in despair. The number of men were as the sands of the sea, and more were still coming from the forest. He had seen the large stacks of arrows made in preparation, but they now seemed insignificant in number to the amount of onrushing men within his view. With the wall now on fire, he surmised that it wouldn't be long until they could enter the town unimpeded.

He thought desperately for some way to stop the invading force.

Even with the power of Lux, he could never cast enough spells to stop them before the town was overtaken.

He began to feel a deep fear and sadness for what awaited him, his family, and all those in Licentia.

Although his family had not been readily accepted by the townspeople, during their preparation time he felt somewhat of a bond with them. There had not been a lot of joy, or even smiling in the last few days, but it had brought a smile to his face when he saw some of the smaller children from town laughing and playing just that morning. His heart ached for those children, what they must be feeling now, and how they would feel once the enemy was upon them.

His mind snapped back to the task at hand and he remembered a spell they used to cool water quickly, conglacior. He shook his head slightly, surely it would not have an effect on those men. He pushed the thought aside, but it seemed to push its way back in, a bit more urgently. Again, he shook his head as if to clear it and get his mind back on the task at hand, and again the word conglacior entered his mind in a soft, persuading voice.

Without knowing why, Japheth instinctively pointed his sword towards the sky and uttered the word, "Conglacior." He waited. Nothing happened. He looked up and saw nothing. Just as he was about to bring Lux down a shaft of bright light shot down and landed in the center of the onrushing men.

When it hit the ground, it made the sound of popping ice on a frozen lake. A white fog, a few feet high spread out almost instantly in all directions. In its wake, everything was a beautiful, frozen, version of its former self.

The invading army was perfectly frozen in place, as was the grass and trees that the fog had contacted. It had also put out the fire along the wall.

The archers slowly lowered their bows and looked out over the scene in wonderment. There were still men coming from the forest towards the town, but they had much difficulty working their way through the entanglement of the soldiers that had been frozen in place. After a few minutes had passed no more men were leaving the forest, but the ones that had, were still slowly making their way towards the town.

Again, Japheth raised Lux, and uttered, "Conglaclor." After a similar pause, the same light came down and sent the same white fog spewing in every direction with identical results. Vesuvius' army of beasts and men had been completely destroyed.

CHAPTER 10

Vesuvius sat concealed in the underbrush of the forest. He had positioned himself to be hidden, yet able to have a perfect view of the battle. Although he was seething after watching his entire army being defeated by a group of untrained commoners, he was collected, as always, on the outside.

He calmly turned to Crag. Crag was a bodyguard of sorts. Although Vesuvius needed no protection, Crag was an intimidating figure whose mere presence would deter most thoughts of an assault on him.

Crag appeared to be some type of animal, most resembling a goat, from the waist down. His torso and upper body were man-like, with the exception of the curled horns growing from his head. Crag was thick and extremely well-muscled, his physique resembling a god from mythology. He was nimble and powerful, but perhaps his most intriguing trait was that he was resistant to magic. Because of this combination of attributes many thought he was Pan, the god of hunters. Vesuvius knew better. Although Crag was a terrifying physical presence, he had a feeble mind and was easily controlled by suggestion.

"Crag," Vesuvius said, "it seems I have underestimated this small village."

Crag only nodded in response.

"I was too quick to dismiss the witch and her family. It seems that she does not have the sword of Merlin, but someone in her household does, that boy," he continued.

"Yes master, but you could defeat him with your staff, I am sure of it," Crag offered.

"Yes, I believe I could, but why would I unnecessarily put myself in harm's way?" Vesuvius mused, not expecting an answer.

Again, Crag nodded his head in understanding.

"If I were to confront him, he could land a lucky blow, and it's not worth the risk at this point."

"Master, you could skip by this village and continue your conquest beyond," Crag suggested.

"I could," Vesuvius said, acknowledging Crag's advice, "but if I am to bring order to mankind it must be complete. I can leave no antagonists to present different ideas. I must insist on obedience. Those that do not accept me cannot be left to oppose me."

"I see," Crag responded.

"What options do I have Crag?" Vesuvius asked.

With a slight shrug of his stout shoulders he answered, "Dragons?"

"Yes Crag, I think dragons would definitely do the trick, but I think we need only send one. If they do have the means to defeat a dragon, I would hate to endanger more than one, they are a scarce animal after all. Crag, signal the others, have them release Forge."

CHAPTER 11

Eli and Abigail pushed through the throng of ecstatic Licentians until they found Japheth. "Son, what happened?" Eli asked.

Japheth still had a look of disbelief on his face as he recounted what had happened. When he finished, his father smiled.

"That was incredible son."

Tabitha approached her gathered family to be filled in as well. Japheth again retold the events to his grandmother.

"Japheth, try that spell on the wall."

Japheth reached out his hand towards the timbers that made up the wall and uttered the spell. Slowly they began to freeze, just as the oak tree had done. He withdrew his hand.

"We need to make sure to record this in the book," she said.

The family conversation was interrupted by a low, steady, pulsating sound. It seemed to be coming from the tops of the trees. It gradually grew louder and louder, and then just above the treetops Japheth saw the source of the sound, a dragon. It flew over the town once and then circled back around. It flew in closer, and as it did it exhaled a stream of fire from its mouth. The fire engulfed the still frozen soldiers and outer wall of Licentia. Everyone at the southern entrance rushed away from the wall and started for the northern entrance to the town. The wall they had built was to keep invaders out, now they feared it would be what would keep them in.

The women and children that had been housed in the center of town where withdrawn from their barricades and hurried towards the north entrance as well.

Men, women, and children poured from the opening at the

north end of the wall. As they did the dragon passed by again and created a wall of fire from the north side of town and around the east side leaving the only route to the forest from the west quarter of Licentia. There was no hole in the wall, and it seemed as if they were trapped.

When Japheth saw the smoke rising from the dragon's second pass on the town, he had reached the center of town. He immediately turned westward. He knew that if the townspeople were to get out of town, they couldn't all get through the north opening in the wall. "Follow me!" he implored as he motioned for the crowd to accompany him westward.

As he meandered his way through town, the wall came into sight. He reached out his hand and spoke the conglacior spell. With Lux at his side to increase his ability, the middle twenty feet of timbers began to freeze.

He concentrated harder as the wall grew closer. The messengers had been able to freeze the oak tree to the point where it became so brittle it shattered under its own weight. He didn't need the wall to get to that point, he just needed it to get close.

When the wall lay just a dozen feet in front of him, he put his hand down and lowered his shoulder. He slammed into the wall and the two timbers he contacted exploded into small fragments of ice.

He stumbled and fell as he passed through the wall. The men behind him followed his lead, blasting into the wall. In just a few moments a twenty-foot hole had been opened in the wall, offering the people another way out of town.

Japheth rose to his feet, looking back at the town. He was bewildered as to why the townsfolk had stopped running. With a sizable opening, they should be rushing towards the forest, the only cover that could offer them any protection.

He turned around only to see that the dragon that had attacked their town now lay directly in front of him, only thirty feet away. Fear gripped him as he stared at the enormous animal.

From deep inside the beast came a thundering bellow. Japheth gagged at the smell of the dragon's breath. It was the hot, putrid smell of rotting flesh. The dragon took in a deep, exaggerated breath as it prepared to spew fire on the escaping Licentians.

Japheth's hours of study immediately jumped to the front of his mind as he recalled the spell to capture a dragon's fire. As the dragon began to exhale, Japheth held his sword in front of him and exclaimed, "Captis!" The fire was not able to spread out far from the dragon's mouth. As it approached the sword it was caught in a vortex and pulled into the sword. Japheth could scarcely bear the blistering heat he felt from the dragon's fire. He closed his eyes to shield them.

As the dragon concluded it seemed to be incensed that nothing had happened. Again, it roared and prepared to unleash its flame upon the townspeople. The moment it stopped to inhale Japheth pointed Lux at the monster before him and burst out, "Exsolvo!"

Instantly the blaze, that had just moments before been captured, flashed towards the dragon, engulfing it in flames. The dragon reared up on its hind legs and fell onto its back. It thrashed wildly as the fire continued to burn. Rolling back up onto its feet it tried to fly away. It had scarcely got into the air when it came crashing back down to the earth, just at the edge of the forest. It struggled to get back onto its feet for a few moments, then fell into a motionless, flaming heap.

Japheth stood there stunned in disbelief of what had just happened. Then he heard the cheering begin from behind him. He turned to see the exuberant, smiling faces of the townspeople. He had delivered them from what they feared was certain, horrible death. Japheth began to smile as well when he saw their joy.

Tabitha, still alert for danger, approached Japheth looking pleased.

"That was quite the display of wizardry young man. Your feats from today are as impressive as any of the stories in our book. But don't let it go to your head," she said with a grin.

"Thanks grandmother," he replied.

Men were stationed as lookouts to keep the town from being completely vulnerable to another attack, but considering the magnitude of the enemy they had just defeated, they considered it highly unlikely. The number of men that had fallen were many times over what even the most powerful king would have at his disposal.

The fires the dragon had created took considerable time to extinguish. When water was poured over the fire it would die momentarily and then just spontaneously spring back to life. Covering it with earth was the only way to put it out and keep it from reigniting. Even when all the apparent fuel had been consumed it continued to burn as if by magic.

The sad work of gathering and burying the dead began immediately. Those that had lost their lives from Licentia where given a ceremony and respectful burial. Most of the enemy soldiers had been incinerated by the dragon's fire. Even the armor and weaponry had been melted by the intense temperatures it produced. The soldiers that had not been turned to ash, were stripped of anything of use and put into a heap in the meadow between town and the forest and prepared for burning.

It was not the way the Licentians would normally handle the dead, but after the attack, they did not want to expend the labor to bury those that would kill or enslave them, and the bodies must still be dealt with.

The Licentians met to decide their next course of action. There was some debate about whether to run or stay.

Tabitha was in favor of leaving the town. "I agree that the wall offers great protection against what we faced today. Men or beasts can be effectively held off by a wall, but if Vesuvius sends an army of wizards, the arrows, and to a lesser degree the wall, won't be much of a hindrance to them. We don't have enough in our family to fend off more than a few at a time. If he sends dragons, we will be an easy target for them if we are all gathered together. Japheth can do only so much."

The rebuttal came from Aaron, "That is true, but I think we still need to stay together and stay put. The wall does offer protection, and if we are out in the open it leaves us much more vulnerable."

Tabitha replied, "I believe we have destroyed the beasts and the men that he had under his command, so if he does attack us it will be with what wizards he has, and he may have more dragons as well. The next time an army approaches it won't be like anything any of us have seen."

"True, but we were able to defeat his messengers without Japheth's help, and he made short work of the dragon. He could do it again," Aaron replied. "He may not even come back to our town after he saw what happened to his forces."

"I highly doubt that," Eli interjected. "He has plans to rule over all of mankind. If we did destroy all his beasts and soldiers he will want retribution. We have just set his plans back years. I have no doubt he will be back."

"Maybe that is where we can get an advantage over him," Tabitha thought out loud. She looked at the others. "If we know he is coming we can make plans, and be prepared to fight and defeat him," she said with increasing confidence.

"Yes," Aaron added. "We need not run. If we work together, we can defeat him."

Tabitha flashed a look of concern. "My only apprehension is that Japheth will end up being his target. After what has happened today, he will realize that Japheth is the only credible threat that this village has."

Thaddeus interjected, "That can also be an advantage to us. He will not be too concerned with anyone else, except maybe you Tabitha, and we can use his focus on Japheth to create a trap for him."

As the group made plans Thaddeus volunteered to be the decoy. He would dress and act as if he were Japheth, and he would stand alongside Tabitha if Vesuvius approached town. After an initial encounter with Vesuvius, the pair would retreat into town. They would lead Vesuvius to a predetermined location, where Japheth would be concealed, and begin another confrontation. Once

Vesuvius had his back to Japheth, he could use Lux to deal a lethal blow to Vesuvius before he would know what had happened.

"Thaddeus," Tabitha said. "For this plan to work you have to be a convincing Japheth."

"Yes, I suppose that is true," he replied.

"Which means," she continued, "you will have to have at least some small ability to use magic. If not, it will not convince Vesuvius, and he will not be fooled our plan."

"No disrespect madam," he said, "but I don't think even you can help me with that. I was hoping by staying near you I would appear to be a wizard in a confrontation."

"I'm a wizard, not a miracle worker," she said with a smile. "You'll have to be able to do something."

The next few days were spent dealing with the dead and wounded, repairing the wall, and preparing for Vesuvius. Thaddeus spent considerable time with Tabitha, striving to learn how to cast the most basic spells, with no success. Just before sundown, three days after Licentia had held off Vesuvius' forces, Japheth approached the practicing Thaddeus and his grandmother. After another failed attempt, Thaddeus hung his head in disappointment and frustration, slightly shaking it back and forth.

"It's no use, I can't do it," he said. "We need to think of something else, possibly another decoy."

"Perhaps," Tabitha said, "but I don't think we should give up just yet. What do you think Japheth?"

"After hearing about what he has lived through already, I don't think there is anything he can't do," Japheth replied.

"Thanks for the assurance Japheth, but I'm afraid this is one area where I am severely lacking, you'd have a better shot using a scarecrow for your deception," he said with a look of defeat on his face.

"Thaddeus, do you think Vesuvius will come himself, or will he send others?" Japheth asked.

"It's hard to say," he replied, "I have never witnessed Vesuvius in defeat, what happens now is anyone's guess. He could avoid the risk of exposing himself to you and send others, or he could be so enraged at what has happened that he shows up in person to deal with you. Whichever option he chooses will tell us a lot about how he views you."

Japheth asked, "What do you mean?"

"If he sees you as a legitimate threat, he would send others, not wanting to endanger himself unless he had no other choice. If after seeing what you did to his armies, he chooses to confront you in person I think the situation is severely grim for all of us. If your power does not give him pause, I don't believe there is a power under heaven that would."

"You keep referring to 'me', but it was all of the town that stood together and defeated his armies," Japheth said.

Tabitha interrupted, "That is true Japheth, but without you, we would not have prevailed. In all sincerity, you are the only one that can possibly match his power. The messengers he sent were more knowledgeable and more skilled at magic than myself, and I'm assuming that he is vastly more powerful than them. He knows he is superior to everyone, everyone that is, except maybe for you."

Japheth had a lot to think about as he made his way to the cottage his family had been assigned to. He lay in bed, not able to sleep for a long while. Lux was removed from his waist and placed on the headboard of his bed, to be readily accessible, just as his grandmother had instructed him. His thoughts lighted on his grandmother's words about him being the focal point of Vesuvius' concern and about him being the only one that could defeat him. As he reluctantly drifted off to sleep the weight of his responsibilities began to bear down upon him.

His sleep was restless, filled with the horrors he had experienced over the last few days, mixed with the new understanding of the magnitude of the burden that he would bear. He awoke early, as usual, and reached a hand over his head to retrieve Lux. He shot up from his bed and gazed at the headboard. He began frantically searching his room. A wave of distress washed over him as he realized that Lux was gone!

CHAPTER 12

Vesuvius and Crag remained in their hiding place as they watched the charred body of Forge burning at the forest's edge. Vesuvius, being highly angered at the loss of his army, was now incensed with fury at the loss of a dragon.

In his mind, he was raging. How dare these insignificant insects stand in his way. They would inevitably die, but just how to do it was the question. Still, he showed no additional hostility in his demeanor.

They had set his plans back years. Without his army he would not be able to overwhelm those that stood in his way. He would have to start again building an army, conditioning those that he conquered to obey him until they would kill their own family if it meant pleasing him.

Crag could sense his master's anger and chose to remain silent. He was not afraid of Vesuvius, he also knew that he was resistant, but not immune to magic. Vesuvius was the only man that had showed Crag respect, albeit counterfeit respect, and for that Crag held high admiration for Vesuvius. He knew that he could become more at Vesuvius' side than he could on his own, so he voluntarily submitted to Vesuvius' wishes.

Crag had come from Ferox. He didn't remember much of the past, but some of his earliest remaining memories were when he lived in that harsh environment. He doesn't remember how, or when he arrived in Ferox. He just remembers the daily struggle to survive, finding food, while trying not to be food for anything else. The constant struggle to sustain himself and being constantly alert for danger had caused him to be extremely perceptive, and also hyper-aggressive. Whoever struck first was often the difference between life and death in Ferox.

He remembers the day when he first met Vesuvius. He was fishing in the drab marshes. He was poised just above a dark pool of water waiting for a fish to come near enough to the surface to be within his reach.

He looked up to see Vesuvius standing before him. He had not heard or sensed anything and seeing something so close to him, startled him. Instinctively he rose and charged. He let out an animal scream as he did.

Vesuvius was ready. He held out his hand and cast the inpulsa spell. He expected the shock to incapacitate the creature before him. The spell hit Crag, with little effect. He stumbled slightly in his charge but continued towards Vesuvius.

The result startled Vesuvius momentarily. As Crag continued charging Vesuvius dropped on one knee and thrust his staff into Crag's abdomen. He lifted his staff upward and easily took Crag off his feet and threw him over his head.

Crag crashed to the ground and skidded a few feet. He quickly got back on his feet and prepared to charge again.

Vesuvius held out a hand in a non-threatening manner and tried to talk to Crag. Crag could not make out much of what he was saying. There was something familiar about the words, but it was nothing he could make sense of. He charged again.

Vesuvius cast the conglacior spell, hopping the freezing of his body would drive Crag to the ground in pain. The spell had no visible effect. He again used his staff and swung it to hit Crag in the side of the head. Crag was prepared this time. He caught the staff in his hand and lowered his shoulder into Vesuvius' chest. Both went to the ground in a heap.

They arose simultaneously, both grasping the staff. Vesuvius held out one hand and cast the ignis spell. Fire leapt from his hand to Crag's body. The fire had little effect. Ignoring the burning sensation caused by the fire, Crag yanked violently on the staff and Vesuvius was pulled off his feet and over Crag's head. Vesuvius hung on and landed on his feet on the other side of Crag. Once he landed, he pulled furiously on the staff. He swung Crag around and slammed him into a tree, cracking the tree and some of Crag's ribs. Crag released the staff and with some difficulty stood.

The staff came down heavily upon his head. The blow stunned him, and he staggered backward. The staff again struck him, this time squarely in the chest and he went to the ground. As he rolled to get up, he felt the staff lodge under his chin and the pressure applied from it cut off his breath. He stood and tried to get Vesuvius off his back, but in a few moments, everything went dark.

He awoke bound and disoriented in Vesuvius' camp. It was there that Vesuvius learned to communicate with him, and eventually convinced him to join with him. That was nearly fifty years ago.

The master turned to his bodyguard, and with the anger visible in his eyes asked, "What shall we do Crag?"

Crag responded with a shake of his head.

"Defeat is not an option. I have planned too well, come too far, and sacrificed too much to stop now. Licentia will pay," Vesuvius vowed. "I have many lifetimes yet to live, to rule, and I will not be stopped by these, or any other people.

"Through most of my life, I have gotten what I wanted by brute force, by imposing my will on others. I think this situation may call for something more subtle. I still do not want to risk confronting that village myself, but what shall I do?"

Crag thought for a moment and answered, "If only you could get the sword Master, then there would be no risk in confronting them."

"Very true Crag, very true. How could I get Merlin's sword?" he asked. "Would you get it for me?"

"If you asked it, I would do it," Crag replied.

"Yes, I know you would, but I think it too dangerous even for you, and I can't afford to lose my next in command. No, I think if we find the right person, they can be … persuaded to get the sword for us. I just must find the right person, someone that has lost much and would fear losing what he has left.

The midnight air was cool. Crag waited just inside the forest, scanning Licentia for any sign of movement. He had grown restless, but his master had assured him that a man would be coming, a man with the sword. Crag continued watching vigilantly for a couple of hours until he finally saw a faint movement.

He could just make out a man sneaking out of Licentia. He watched as he slowly made his way through the tall grass that surrounded the town. When the man reached the forest, he made his way to a large dead pine tree. Crag continued watching as the man leaned a sword on the tree. The man looked up and scanned the forest. It was unnaturally quiet and his voice, though little more than a whisper, seemed to reverberate throughout the dark woods.

"Vesuvius, I have done as you have commanded, now I ask that you follow through on your promise." With that, the man turned and sneaked back into the town.

Crag waited for him to get all the way back before he moved. He walked to the tree and grasped the sword. It seemed like an ordinary sword and Crag immediately wondered if it was a counterfeit. He withdrew it from its scabbard and admired its perfect construction. There was something different about this weapon, and upon examining it he was satisfied that it was the sword that his master desired.

Crag walked silently through the forest until he came to Vesuvius' camp. He walked into the tent to find Vesuvius reading an ancient book by candlelight. He looked up from his book at Crag and smiled wickedly.

"You move so silently through the brush that I believe you could sneak up on the devil himself Crag. Do you have it?"

Crag nodded his head and returned a crooked smile.

"Perfect, in the morning we'll pack up camp, and head for the castle where we will prepare for another assault on Licentia. Without the sword, we will crush those putrescent peasants, and they will be forgotten to history."

CHAPTER 13

Japheth frantically left his room and began searching the house. When Eli and Abigail saw his panicked state, they questioned him.

"Japheth, what is wrong?" his mother asked.

Japheth looked up, his face filled with fear, "Lux is gone."

Eli asked, "Are you sure?"

"Yes, I put it on the headboard, just as I do every night. When I awoke this morning, it was gone," he responded.

"How can this be?" Tabitha said from behind Japheth. "Did we have any visitors last night?"

"No," Abigail said, "no one."

"Who could have taken it? Who would want to take it?" Tabitha asked to no one in particular. "Everyone in this town owes their life to Japheth and that sword, why would someone take it?"

"I don't know," Japheth replied, "but it's gone."

Eli added, "Let's not panic, I'll check with the watchmen to see if they noticed anyone leaving town. If they haven't, the sword is still here, and we may be able to discover who has taken it. If we continue to act like nothing is wrong, we may be able to flush the culprit out."

Tabitha thought for a moment and then agreed. "Yes, but we cannot spend many days here. If we are indeed without Lux, we cannot possibly face Vesuvius and we must flee."

The family went about their day as if nothing was amiss. Tabitha continued to work with Thaddeus, but her urgency for him to be successful was not there, and he noticed.

"What is wrong Tabitha? You seem to have lost some of your fire for teaching me the skills of wizardry," he asked.

"Oh, nothing is wrong," she countered, "I just have a lot on my mind."

"You've always got a lot on your mind, it's almost like you never stop thinking. It must be something else, something more pressing," Thaddeus returned. "Have you lost faith in me, as I have myself?" he asked.

"No," she said, "It's not that." She paused, deep in thought, contemplating the ramifications of telling Thaddeus their secret.

"Then what is it?" he pressed. "Something is wrong, you can trust me, please share."

There was a long, uncomfortable pause before she replied. "Lux has been taken."

The shock in Thaddeus' face lasted only moments before he asked, "By whom?"

"We don't know," she answered, "but we think it is still in Licentia. We haven't told anyone but our family, hoping we can determine who has it. If we can't find the guilty party in a few days, we may push for everyone to leave town. We have no chance against Vesuvius without it."

"What do you need me to do?" Thaddeus asked.

"Right now, just keep your eyes and ears open to anything that seems suspicious," she said, "if we can't find any clues, we'll have to come clean with the community. Right now, we think this is our best chance of getting it back."

Thaddeus and Tabitha decided to cut their training short for the day to spend more time looking for any indication of who may have Lux.

The entire family returned to their cottage earlier than normal, anxious to share, or hear, what had been learned throughout the day.

Tabitha opened the conversation, "I didn't come across anything suspicious today."

"Nor did I," said Eli.

"Apparently no one did," Abigail added.

Japheth said, "I sure hope we are right about Lux still being here."

"I also told Thaddeus about what has happened," Tabitha said.

"I thought we were keeping that knowledge within the family," Deborah commented, slightly irked.

"We were, but I think Thaddeus can be trusted, and one more set of alert eyes and ears can only help," Tabitha responded.

Deborah nodded her head in reluctant agreement and then changed the subject. "I think we should begin to make preparations if we have to confront Vesuvius without Lux."

"If we don't have Lux, we won't confront Vesuvius," Tabitha interrupted. "He is far too powerful for us to challenge, we would stand no chance."

Deborah continued with her thought, "We may not desire a confrontation, but we may not have a choice."

Tabitha looked quizzically at Deborah and asked, "What do you have in mind?"

With a look of determination in her eyes, Deborah responded with a single word, "Dragonsbane."

"Absolutely not," Tabitha protested. "It is far too dangerous for us to use."

Deborah countered, "It is dangerous, but so is Vesuvius. If we don't have something extreme at our disposal, he will crush us like bugs. If we can't find Lux, we need dragonsbane to have any kind of a fighting chance."

Tabitha thought for a long moment and then said, "I suppose you are right, if we don't have Lux it probably doesn't matter what we have, but dragonsbane would give us something that could work against a dragon, and perhaps against Vesuvius himself. I am very hesitant to try to concoct it into a usable form, but I'm guessing you feel equal to the challenge."

"Yes, I do. I know it is dangerous, but I feel confident that if I am careful, I can get it dried and ready in a couple of days," Abigail explained. "I have seen some growing in the forest not far from here."

"How will we carry it?" Adam asked.

"In dragon skin," Tabitha answered.

"And where are we going to get dragon skin?" Adam asked again.

"From the dragon that Japheth killed," was her reply. "The skin of a dragon does not burn. Though the fire killed it, its skin is still intact. We need to dig up what is left of the carcass, cut out some of the hide, soften it, and turn it into small carrying pouches."

Deborah smiled triumphantly and said, "Well that settles it then, tomorrow I'll start out for the dragonsbane. Adam and Eli can get enough of the dragon's hide to make the necessary pouches."

The following day went much as the day before. The family spent their day looking and listening for any clues that would lead them to whoever had taken Lux. Deborah successfully collected a large bundle of dragonsbane for drying. Adam and Eli cut multiple large sections of the dragon's skin to produce the pouches they would need to carry the incendiary plant.

"Aunt Deborah," Japheth asked, "how are you going to dry the dragonsbane out in time to use it if Vesuvius comes against us? Doesn't it take a long time for a plant to dry out?"

"Yes, it does," she answered, "but if you know the right spell you can dry it out almost immediately."

"Really?" Japheth asked skeptically.

"Of course," she replied cheerfully. "What good is it to be a wizard if you have to do everything the hard way?"

There was a knock at the door. When Eli opened it, Thaddeus stepped through and into the cottage.

He looked at the assembled family, "Any news?" he inquired.

Tabitha shook her head and said, "None yet, and you?"

"Sadly, I haven't observed anything out of the ordinary," he returned. "Do we want to try it for one more day, or should we plan on informing everyone else?"

Tabitha sat in contemplation for a few moments and then answered, "I think we should try one more day. We have gathered some drangonsbane and will have it prepared by the end of the day tomorrow. If we don't have any clues as to the location of Lux, we can inform the town of the situation and make additional plans at that point."

Thaddeus nodded his head in agreement, "Very well, I'll see you tomorrow." He left as quickly as he had come in.

"Grandmother, who is going to prepare the dragonsbane?" Japheth asked.

"Your aunt Deborah and I," was her reply.

"Isn't it dangerous?" he asked.

"Yes it is, but if great care is taken everything should go alright," Tabitha explained.

"Everything will go well," Deborah added, "but I will be the only one handling and preparing the dragonsbane."

Tabitha began to protest but was cut off by Deborah.

"Mother, you are a vastly superior wizard to me, but I have many times over the experience of preparing ingredients and mixing potions. If anyone can prepare the dragonsbane without an incident it is me, putting you in harm's way is not worth the risk. I can have it all prepared myself tomorrow. We need to make sure we have as many pouches made as possible. Your efforts would be better utilized in helping with those."

Tabitha ended any further objection she may have had and simply agreed saying, "You're right."

As the family went to bed that night there was an uneasy apprehension about what the coming day would bring.

That morning the family awoke early. Deborah began the perilous task of drying and preparing the dragonsbane in an isolated room. Tabitha, Abigail, and some of the older grandchildren began cutting, softening, and sewing the dragon's hide into pouches that would house the searing plant once it was ready. The men in the family headed back out into town to help with repairs and preparations for whatever may be coming, but more importantly to look for any clues that may lead them to Lux's location.

Near the end of the day, the family congregated back at their cottage. As Japheth came in, he noticed about thirty pouches made from the dragon's skin sitting on a shelf, each filled about halfway with the caustic powder that would hopefully give them an advantage against Vesuvius if they were to encounter him.

His aunt Deborah sat at the table with her hands in a bucket of water with Adam gently rubbing her shoulders.

"What happened, are you alright?" Japheth asked.

Deborah forced a smile as she looked at him and said, "Oh nothing too bad, I'll be alright."

Tabitha snorted in disgust. "She won't be alright. She got some of the powder on her hands while she was preparing the dragonsbane. Instead of stopping, she continued and got more and more of it on her. Wherever it came in contact with her skin it will burn for the rest of her life."

"Unless we can find an antidote?" Japheth asked.

Tabitha explained, "Yes, but I don't know how we will ever find one, or if there even is one. She has made a monumental personal sacrifice for us this day. From what I understand of dragonsbane, the constant pain it causes will drive the sufferer mad."

Adam spoke up, "But we won't let that happen will we."

Deborah, still forcing a smile, said, "I guess as a last resort we could remove my hands."

"That is not funny Deborah," Tabitha snapped. "Now that she is in constant pain, she won't be able to use her powers either. It takes concentration to use magic, and with that level of pain she may never cast another spell."

Japheth suggested, "What about the conglacior spell, could that possibly give her some relief?"

"Perhaps," Tabitha said after some contemplation, "but it must be used very delicately. If the spell is cast with too much force it could cause frostbite and she would lose her hands." Tabitha looked at Deborah and asked, "Would you like me to try?"

Deborah nodded her head and said, "Yes, I believe I would."

Tabitha took Deborah's hands in hers. As she touched them Deborah winced in pain. Tabitha closed her eyes to concentrate and subtly spoke the conglacior spell. As she did Deborah let out a sigh of reprieve, and her entire body relaxed.

"Oh thank you," Deborah said.

Tabitha got up and moved to Abigail. "We'll have to see how

long the relief lasts. I don't think this will be a long-term solution, but it will suffice for now."

Just then Thaddeus burst through the door, an urgent look in his eyes. "I think I may have found who has taken Lux!"

CHAPTER 14

Eli and Japheth hastily followed Thaddeus out of the cottage, and the trio rushed through the streets of Licentia as Thaddeus explained.

"I noticed a man yesterday making the argument that we should leave Licentia. I don't believe he was of that mindset shortly after the battle. There were not many who believed that to be our best course of action. I dismissed it, but today he was extremely adamant that we leave as soon as possible. When he couldn't change any people's opinion, he got angry and belligerent. He kept saying he was certain that Vesuvius was coming soon. He made quite a spectacle of himself.

"When he noticed me, he came and appealed to me to persuade the townspeople to leave. I told him that I wasn't leaving even if everyone else did because I knew Vesuvius would come, and if he wanted someone to side with him, he'd better look elsewhere.

"I trailed him for a while, and not long ago he slumped to the ground muttering to himself. It was hard to make out what he was saying but I managed to hear something about betraying the entire town. I waited for him to go home so I would know where to find him. As soon as he did, I came to get you."

They quickly reached a small home as Thaddeus finished with the details.

Eli lifted his hand and battered the small door in front of him.

A meek voice came from the other side. "Who is there?"

"It is Eli, I need to speak with you at once," he said in a tone that did not hide his intentions.

"I'm tired, please leave me alone," the voice returned.

"I will not ask again, if you do not open this door immediately, I will turn it into splinters."

Eli waited for a few brief moments and then backed up to prepare to kick in the door when he heard the latch on the other side being opened. The door slowly opened to reveal a man that Eli recognized as being right in the middle of the fighting during the great battle. As he gazed upon the man, he remembered his name, James.

This recollection softened Eli ever so slightly. "May we come in?" he asked in a way that was clearly not a question. The man dropped his head, turned into the room and submissively waved them in. The three men entered the room and closed the door behind them.

"I am not one to mince words, so I'll get right to the gist of our visit," Eli announced. "We have reason to believe that you know where Lux is, is this true?"

The man turned and sat silently, never lifting his gaze from the floor. He began talking to himself as much as to the men who had called on him. "He told me he would give me my son back if I brought him the sword. I should have known he is a liar."

"Who has your son?" Thaddeus asked.

James replied in a subdued sob, "No one, but I thought Vesuvius had him."

"How did this happen?" Eli asked.

James took some time to compose himself before he began his tale. "The night after the great battle I had extremely restless sleep. Vesuvius came to me in a dream. He told me he had taken my only son, and that he had caused a deep sleep to come upon all your household. He would deliver my son to me only if I sneaked into your cottage, stole Lux, and delivered it to him in the forest outside of town. In the dream, he said if he did not have the sword by morning, I would never see my son again. If I did, my son would be returned to me.

"I awoke in a panic and I bolted into my son's room to find him gone. I frantically searched the house, but he was nowhere to be found. I felt like I had no choice, so I crept to your cottage and into Japheth's room. I got the sword and left town.

"He was right, everyone in your house was eerily asleep. I could have broken a dish on the floor, and it wouldn't have roused you.

"When I returned home, I went again into my son's room to find him asleep in bed. Hurriedly I crossed his room and embraced him. He was startled by my actions and asked me what was wrong. I rehearsed to him my dream, and what I had done that night. He looked quizzically at me and told me he had not been taken but in his bed all night.

"I think Vesuvius had some type of control over my mind and made me think that my son was gone when he was not, and he tricked me into getting the sword for him.

"My wife died giving birth to him. He is my only child and my only piece of her that I have. The thought of losing him terrified me."

In a flash, Eli crossed the room and jerked the man to his feet. Holding him up by his shirt he looked into his tear-filled eyes. "How could you!" he demanded. "You've killed us all!" Eli began to reach for his sword when his hand was stopped by Thaddeus'.

"Eli," he said. "Stop! How did you feel when Japheth went into battle? Did you worry that you might never see him again?"

Thaddeus' words made Eli pause. He continued, "Remember those feelings, that's what this man went through, surely you can understand why he did what he did."

Eli loosened his grip on the man and his sword. He let him fall to the ground. Eli, Thaddeus, and Japheth began the trip back to their cottage to inform the rest of the family about what they had learned.

When Eli had finished recounting what James had told him the family sat in silence. Each person sat in disbelief as the significance of what had happened sunk in. Not only did they not have Lux, but it was in Vesuvius' possession. Any chance they believed they had of prevailing was quickly fading.

Japheth was the first to volunteer his thoughts. "We could run."

"We could," Tabitha said, "but I doubt it would do any good. We only have a few days at most before Vesuvius comes. We couldn't put enough distance between us and this place to hide from him."

Abigail added, "She's right we have to stay and fight."

"How can we?" Japheth asked. "Without Lux one dragon could destroy all of us."

Each family member realized the truthfulness of his words. Deborah sat, her hands beginning to get uncomfortably warm again when she spoke. "Things do not look good, but we do have an advantage with the dragonsbane. If we could somehow surprise Vesuvius with it, we could have a chance."

"I'm doubtful that we would be successful," Tabitha said.

"But what other options do we have?" Deborah asked.

"None," Eli replied. "We can't move this big of a group of people fast enough to run. We are going to have to fight him at some point, whether that be here, or on the run. We just as well start planning now."

"Do we tell everyone else?" Japheth asked.

"I think we need to," Tabitha answered. "If we are going to make some grand plan, we will need everyone involved. I think it would be best to have the basic idea of what we want to do before we inform the town."

"I agree," Thaddeus said. "If we have something for them to concentrate on and work towards it will give them confidence, and maybe some hope."

The family sat up a good portion of the night deliberating their options before agreeing on their best course of action.

Tabitha was the first one up, and she quickly roused everyone else. They hurriedly ate breakfast and got out into town before anyone else was out and engaged in the day's labors. Each member of the family was assigned a section of town to cover, they were to invite the townspeople to the town square to hear the news and their plan. This task was completed quickly, and the family gathered in the heart of Licentia and waited for everyone else to arrive.

When it looked as though everyone that was going to come was there Eli arose and spoke.

"Fellow Licentians, we have discouraging news. Lux has been stolen and it is in Vesuvius' possession." He paused for the gathered crowd to comprehend the significance of what he had just told them. Before he could continue, the gathering burst into an uproar of questions.

"Who stole it? How was it stolen? How could you let it happen?" These were just a few of the barrage of questions thrown at the family in an instant.

Tabitha could see the rising anxiety of the crowd and that things were going to get quickly out of hand. The crowd had to be quieted, and order restored. She stepped forward and clapped her hands. The resulting sound was comparable to the sound a massive tree makes as it falls to the ground. In response, the group stilled.

Eli spoke again, "We do not have much time to prepare. We believe Vesuvius will be upon us in a matter of days, if that. We can fill you in on any details we have as we begin preparations, but it is imperative that we decide on a course of action and move towards it as soon as possible.

"When we learned Lux had been taken, we did not inform anyone. Our intention in not telling anyone was to look for clues as to who may have taken it. After a few days we were able to find that individual, and also what had been done with the sword. That is how we know Vesuvius has it."

Eli was interrupted by a multiplicity of people all demanding to know who had stolen the sword. Eli searched the crowd until his eyes lighted upon James. As he looked at him, he remembered how bravely he had fought, and the loss he had suffered.

Still looking upon him Eli said, "Who has stolen the sword is of no importance, but the individual responsible for stealing Lux is no longer among us, and that is all I will say about it."

This answer did not pacify the crowd, and they began to press for more answers. Again, the crowd was beginning to work themselves into a frenzy when Tabitha again stepped forward and clapped her hands together. The resulting sound was near to the sound, and magnitude of a large clap of thunder. Nearly everyone in the crowd stopped to cover their ears.

Eli began again, "Our chances against Vesuvius are not good, but we do have one asset that may be enough of a help for us to defeat him. When the sword was stolen, we immediately began to procure, and prepare dragonsbane.

"It is a rare plant that when dried and ground to a powder has an insatiable burning effect on whatever it comes into contact with. It is the only thing we know of that would have any effect on a dragon, if you can pierce its skin with it.

"Deborah has gone to great pains to concoct it, and as a result will suffer for the remainder of her life. This she has done to give us a chance to defend ourselves against a superior enemy.

"What we propose is to station archers out around the town concealed in the forest, and more inside the town, with the dragonsbane. When Vesuvius arrives, we can then coat our arrowheads with the dragonsbane and use them to defeat dragon, wizard, or whatever man or beast he may have under his command."

Presenting a plan to the townsfolk for the dilemma they faced seemed to move their thoughts from a lynching to their own self-preservation. A meeting was then held to decide who the archers would be, and where they would be stationed.

Once this was decided all the designated men were given a pouch of the dragonsbane, and instructions on how to use it. The arrowheads could not be coated with the powder very far in advance of using them. Each archer was also given a ball of tree sap.

Once Vesuvius made his presence known the archers would apply some sap to the arrowhead and then dip it in the pouch. Once the drangonsbane was applied to the arrow the archer had about a half an hour before the arrowhead would get hot enough to make the shaft begin to smoke.

It was imperative that the archers in the forest remain hidden. Each archer was given a cloak that had twigs and brush sewn into it to camouflage them in the forest. They were also given enough provisions so that they could remain in the forest for days at a time if necessary so they would not reveal their hiding places.

Half of the archers were to be within the walls of Licentia, hidden among the homes. If whatever threat they faced got inside the walls, they hoped it would put them in a better position to combat the enemy they faced.

CHAPTER 15

As Eli and Japheth made final preparations to take their places outside of the wall, there was a faint knock at the door. When Japheth opened it, James stood in the open doorway. Meekly he asked, "May I come in?"

Japheth turned to the side and motioned for him to come in. As he entered, the house became silent. James approached Eli, head down. He looked up at Eli and asked, "Why did you lie? Why didn't you tell them I had taken your sword? I was prepared to answer for what I have done to this town."

Eli grabbed James by the shoulders and said, "I didn't lie. The man who took Lux no longer exists. That man is dead. The man that thought Vesuvius could be believed is no more. You learned an unfortunate lesson at what I feel will be a terrible price. My hope is that moving forward you will help look after my family as you would your own."

A tear fell down James' face. "Thank you, thank you all for your forgiveness," he said as he looked over their family. "I can never repay your kindness, but I will give all that I have in the attempt." With that James turned and walked back through the door.

<hr>

The men that were to be outside of the wall met together for final instructions before they were all but isolated until Vesuvius returned. Aaron took charge.

"You may very well be our best hope of survival. Once you are secreted in the forest you are to move as little as possible, we don't know where the eyes and ears of Vesuvius may be. You must wait with complete patience, our survival may depend on it.

"You are spaced so that there will be very few places that they can make an assault on the town that they are not within range of someone's arrows. No matter what happens we have to make an attack on Vesuvius himself. We can't afford to lose the element of surprise on men, wizards, or even dragons. Vesuvius is the head of the snake, if we cut it off the body dies.

"If we must, we will engage Vesuvius to give you time to surprise him. The wizards will be stationed around the wall to provide all the support they can.

"If we are victorious this day we can return to our normal lives, to live and let live. If we are not able to prevail, I believe it better that we perish than be brought into servitude. Men of Licentia live free or die with courage!"

The men departed to their predetermined hiding places to wait for whatever dangers they would face. Tabitha watched as many men as she could to see exactly where they would be hidden, the information may prove pivotal in the coming days.

The people of Licentia waited in anticipation all that day, but things remained calm. The same thing happened the next day, and the next. The men stationed just inside the forest were low on, if not out of, food and water by now. The isolation was difficult to bear as well. Three days of sitting and waiting was taking its toll on them mentally.

Every possible scenario they could think of ran through their heads over and over. Day upon day of monotony, coupled with dwindling provisions began to diminish the resolve that they set out with. Most of the men remained firm, but there were a few that left their posts and went back into Licentia, and if things remained uneventful it wouldn't be long until they would all have to return.

Eli was stationed perfectly to be hidden but have a perfect view of the town. One of the men that had returned to town had been on his left. Japheth was to his right. That was one condition of Japheth being allowed to be one of the assigned archers.

Eli knew he was more capable than most of the other men assigned, but he wanted his son close, so he could protect him.

Just as dusk was approaching on the fourth day there was a
familiar low, steady, pulsating sound that infused fear into each individual as the realization of what created it sunk in.

A single dragon slowly came into view over the treetops. A few
brief moments later another was visible, then another, and finally
a fourth.

Upon hearing the sound Eli prepared two arrows with tree sap
but decided to wait on applying the dragonsbane.

As they drew closer it appeared as if figures were riding atop
two of the dragons. They circled the town a few times, slowed, and
landed. They landed closer to town than had been anticipated.
They had assumed if dragons did come, they would be as close to
the forest as possible to be out of range of any archers, or wizards.
They assumed this would be to their advantage because it would
put them well within range of their archers concealed in the forest.

As Eli quickly studied the dragon that had landed to his left, he
recognized Vesuvius. He also realized that he would have to sneak
through the tall gas to get close enough to him to get a reliable
shot. The man to his left had gone back to town, if Vesuvius was to
be surprised it would have to be him.

Immediately he removed his cloak, the camouflage that had
been added would not be effective in the open grass. He began to
crawl on his stomach through the grass towards Vesuvius, but he
knew it would take him some time. He only hoped that Vesuvius
could be stalled long enough for him to get within range.

As the dragon landed Tabitha too realized that it was Vesuvius
that had ridden it here and that Eli would be the closest archer and
would need some time to get close enough for a trustworthy shot.

Vesuvius stood up on the dragon he was on and addressed the
town, as he did Tabitha quickly sought to make her way onto a rooftop to be able to both hear, address, and confront him.

"I admire your fortitude, your drive, and your tenacity. This
town has given me more of a fight than the mightiest kingdoms

I have conquered. I have simply rolled over any opposition I have faced, until this town. You have been a thorn in my side, a festering sliver, and I am about to pluck you out. While you have shown successful resistance, it will be shown to be fruitless because you will share the same fate as all those that have opposed me."

"Are you sure about that?" Tabitha asked as she scaled to the peak of the roof. "I seem to recall that not too long ago a dragon burned at the edge of this forest. What makes you think we can't do it again?" Tabitha was bluffing, she was trying to get into some type of confrontation that would buy Eli enough time to get close enough for a shot.

Vesuvius began laughing as he held up the sword that Crag had brought him their last night in the forest surrounding Licentia.

"Because witch, I have your sword. I witnessed firsthand the power it has, but I also know that without it you are powerless against me and these magnificent beasts, you will fall before me!"

Tabitha returned the laugh accompanied with a smile. "That is not the Sword of Merlin."

Before she could continue Vesuvius cut her off, "Liar! If it is not, where is your champion? Where is the man that defeated my armies? Why is he not here now?"

Tabitha answered, still smiling, "He is on his way."

Her comment caused a moment of pause in Vesuvius, and she noticed it from the change in his countenance, so she continued calmly. "He will come and destroy you, but perhaps he will spare the dragons. It has been generations since they have been seen. Something so rare shouldn't be killed so hastily."

Vesuvius' anger boiled to the surface at her defiance, yet he did not let it show. "Tell me your champions name, that I may know it before he meets his demise."

Now it was Tabitha that was hesitant. She did not want to reveal Japheth's name. Vesuvius noticed the change in Tabitha.

"I see that you are reluctant. That tells me that he is dear to you, perhaps a close family member, and you are afraid that once I find out his name, he will no longer be safe. It also tells me that you truly fear me and that I most likely have your sword."

Tabitha continued to stall. "If that is the sword, tell me, have you learned to use it?" She was trying to plant doubt in Vesuvius, once again, with her question.

It did not have her desired effect. Vesuvius had read Tabitha's body language, and the things that she wouldn't say, which made him quite confident in his reading of the situation. Knowing that he was not in any danger to speak of, he took this moment to revel in his inevitable triumph.

Calmly, Vesuvius replied as he looked over Lux. "I have not learned how to use it. According to the legend it is a very mysterious weapon and using it can be difficult. Luckily for me, I have lifetimes yet to live and to discover its secrets. Once I have unlocked them, I will be invincible, and perhaps instead of being nearly immortal I will discover how to completely cheat death."

His change triggered panic in Tabitha. She could sense that a conflict would happen in the next few moments. She also knew that Eli had not had time to close the gap enough to get a shot at Vesuvius.

"Ignis! Inpulsa! Conglacior! Glacies!" Tabitha tried to surprise Vesuvius with spells cast in rapid succession. He easily dispelled each one. She paused, her intent was not to defeat Vesuvius but to stall for time. She knew Eli would be watching and this would hopefully signal him that there was no more time.

Vesuvius looked at Tabitha with contempt. "Is that your best? Is that all you can muster? Did you think that that pitiful display of amateurish magic would be successful against me? I must admit that I have lost what little respect I had for you. I see that without your sword you people are nothing. It cheapens the victory somewhat for me, but I care little about that. In a matter of minutes, your town will be ablaze with the unquenchable fire of these dragons and you will be erased from history, but I will take care of you first."

Vesuvius shot a massive shock wave towards Tabitha. She used the clipeum spell to absorb the shock. She then used the impetus spell, which created an intense burst of wind that sent the dragon stumbling back slightly.

Vesuvius shot fire in an upward arc towards her. She easily dissipated the flame.

"Enough!" he yelled. Vesuvius reached out his hand, palm up, and drew his fingers inward. As he did Tabitha dropped to the roof, in anguish.

Eli had seen Tabitha try her magic against Vesuvius and he believed that a confrontation was at hand. He was too far to get a confident shot on Vesuvius, but he did believe he could hit his dragon from where he was. He rolled to his back and inserted the two arrowheads into the pouch of dragonsbane, preparing to fire. He would aim for Vesuvius, but he would aim low so that if he missed, he would most likely hit the dragon.

Just as Vesuvius had released his spell from Tabitha and was about to direct his dragon to flood the town with fire, Eli moved to his knees, took aim at Vesuvius and released his two arrows in quick succession.

The first arrow hit the dragon in the back, just behind Vesuvius' leg. This caused the dragon to recoil slightly. The movement cause Vesuvius to pause in his command to the dragon. The second arrow hit somewhat lower than the first which triggered another flinch from the dragon, and an additional delay from Vesuvius.

Those brief pauses were all that was needed for the effect of the dragonsbane to be felt. The dragon began to back up in jerky motions. It turned its head to see the cause of its increasing discomfort. As the pain worsened it began to jerk, kick, and buck. The unanticipated behavior of the dragon surprised Vesuvius who was not ready. A few seconds into the dragon's spasms Vesuvius was thrown from the dragons back to the ground.

Eli noticed that he landed awkwardly on his side, perhaps landing on a rock. Vesuvius arose and grasped his side, apparently in pain.

Eli nocked another arrow and quickly shot it in the direction of Vesuvius. Having lost the element of surprise Vesuvius was prepared. The arrow crumbled in midflight. Vesuvius located Eli and was about to counter-attack when the dragon, being increasingly agitated by the dragonsbane, began to spit fire randomly.

The first streams of fire leapt towards the general direction of where Tabitha had been. Then as the dragon began turning in circles the fire seemed to be everywhere.

Through the heat and the smoke, Eli watched Vesuvius as he ran towards the forest, still gripping his side. Eli followed, hoping he could catch him and put an end to this conflict for good.

The dragon, now wild and delirious, took off and began flying in the direction in which it had come. The two dragons without riders followed. Only Crag and the dragon he commanded remained. Unsure of what had transpired, Crag thought for a few moments, then commanded his dragon to spew fire upon the town. It quickly discharged the fire as it moved its head from right to left across the town.

When it had finished, Crag commanded it to leave as well. Then just as quickly as they had come, they were gone.

Eli was continuing to trail Vesuvius through the trees but was not gaining as quickly as he had anticipated.

Japheth, who had also been making his way towards Vesuvius, had not been nearly as close as his father when Eli had made his attack. From where he was in the grass he watched as Vesuvius was thrown from his dragon. He did not notice Vesuvius being hurt as he landed, his attention was on an item that glimmered in the fading sun as it tumbled towards the ground. He was too far away to be sure of what it was. Quickly he weaved his way around the patches of fire among the tall grass of the meadow around Licentia until he approached the area where the item fell.

When his eyes lighted upon it he was filled with a deep sense of relief. There in the burnt grass of the meadow lay Lux. He immediately seized it and turned to look in the direction his father had gone. He knew his father would stand little chance by himself if he was pursuing Vesuvius.

As he began following his father his body began to tingle and the world around him seemed to slow. He knew in a matter of minutes he would have to confront Vesuvius and he must have a plan to defeat him.

CHAPTER 16

As Japheth sped in the direction his father had gone in pursuit of Vesuvius, his mind began to race for ideas of how he could possibly defeat him. From what he had gathered it did seem like Vesuvius found satisfaction in gloating in his victories.

As he thought about this, an idea came into his mind. Vesuvius is the most powerful individual that Japheth had ever heard of, and few things could match that power, except maybe for the forces of nature. If he could get Vesuvius to handle Lux while he was in the vicinity, he could try to call down lightning with the fulgur spell. The power of that spell had defeated wizards in times past, so he reasoned it could do the same now. The only worry he had was that he would be too close to Vesuvius when he called down lightning, and he would be destroyed as well.

He had just decided on what to try when he came upon his father, leaning with his back against a tree, in obvious pain.

⊷⊷⊷◉⊷⊷

It had taken Eli a few minutes to catch Vesuvius, and once he had, he wished he hadn't. He drew an arrow back in his bow and fired. Just before he released, Vesuvius turned and the arrow turned to powder before it had cleared the end of his bow.

Eli realized that arrows were useless, the only other options he had was his sword and a couple of throwing knives.

By instinct, he darted behind a tree to provide himself some cover.

Vesuvius addressed Eli, "Why hide? You followed me, what did you hope to accomplish? I would never have stopped coming against your people, but you didn't need to seek me out. Now you will die."

The tree he was hiding behind began quickly getting cold. In a few more moments it cracked and exploded into fragments of ice.

Eli dove and rolled behind another tree.

This time the tree erupted in flames.

Eli began to retreat into the forest. As he ran through a small clearing, he was hit with a terrible shock that sent him to the ground. His body ached, but the fear of facing Vesuvius alone compelled him to his feet. Again he sought refuge behind a tree, but he was in too much pain to run, all he could do was lean back against the tree and wait for whatever would come.

As he was giving in to despair, he saw his son speeding towards him.

⟫⟪(0)⟫⟪

Japheth stopped beside his father.

"Son, don't try to fight him, he is much too powerful."

Eli's gaze fell to his son's hand, which held Lux. Eli tried to smile and said, "Even with that sword you are no match for him. I will try to hold him off while you get back to town."

Japheth looked at his father and replied, "I can't run. I wouldn't leave you to the wolves, and I won't leave you to Vesuvius. I can beat him father, I have a plan. You need to get away from here quickly if you don't want to die a spectacular death."

Eli could sense the confidence in his son, and see the smoke rising from Licentia. He debated only momentarily what to do. As he looked at his son, he knew he could trust him, then he started towards town. Japheth slowly strolled into the clearing.

Vesuvius waited at the opposite edge of the small field. He looked with malice at Japheth and spoke to him condescendingly.

"Well boy, I see that you have retrieved your beloved sword. Little good it will do you."

Japheth cut Vesuvius off. "I don't need this sword to defeat a witch like you." Japheth chose his words carefully to show as much contempt as possible.

Vesuvius, who never let his anger show, exploded with rage. "You insolent wretch! I am the most powerful being in this or any other land! All who survive my wrath will bow to me, but you will not be one of them!"

Japheth passively turned Lux over in his hand and stuck it into the ground. He then moved around the clearing away from the sword.

Japheth's words and actions startled Vesuvius. How could this boy be so confident? Was he trying to trick him? Vesuvius continued watching Japheth, waiting for him to do something so he could better assess his situation.

Vesuvius mirrored his movements around the open field.

Japheth stopped, peered at Vesuvius and began casting inpulsa spells one after another. The shocks were easily countered by Vesuvius. Then he tried the caecus spell to try to blind him. Vesuvius had already made himself resistant to that spell, as he had his entire army after Japheth had used it against the animals he had under his control.

When that was unsuccessful Japheth tried the conglacior spell, which was also easily dismissed. Japheth's behavior was puzzling to Vesuvius. He reasoned that he couldn't possibly be trying to be successful with these spells.

Japheth switched to the ignis spell, which he was more comfortable with than the other spells, and as a result, they had a little more intensity, but the flames were easily extinguished.

As Vesuvius countered these spells, he began to laugh. "This is the best you can do?" he said as he chuckled.

That was what Japheth was waiting for. He knew that Vesuvius would get overconfident, and that is when he would have his chance.

Japheth pulled a throwing knife from its sheath, and as he had practiced it with his grandmother, he bound the ignis spell to the knife with the apio spell as he threw it. He aimed for Vesuvius' chest but missed just to the side.

Vesuvius only saw another ball of fire speeding towards him. As he countered the spell the ball dissipated but the knife did not. He noticed something different an instant before the knife stuck into his outstretched hand.

Japheth had thrown the knife with such force that it penetrated his hand and protruded out the backside.

Vesuvius recoiled his hand in pain.

Japheth had cast an inpulsa spell immediately after he threw the knife. As a result, when Vesuvius had brought his hand down, he was momentarily vulnerable, and the shock hit him.

Vesuvius fell to the ground in agony, yet he forced himself to focus his anger on Japheth. He made a backhanding motion towards Japheth causing him to go sailing backward and he slammed violently into a tree, nearly knocking him unconscious.

He pulled the knife from his hand and stood. His eyes turned black with hate, and anger filled his soul. Through gritted teeth he cursed Japheth. He reached out his hand, palm up with blood dripping from it, and drew his fingers inward.

Japheth, still stunned from striking the tree, felt as if he was being crushed. He couldn't move, he couldn't even speak. At this point, Japheth was hoping this is when Vesuvius would go get the sword and he could carry out his plan.

Instead, Vesuvius walked over to where Japheth lay helpless on the ground. With his unoccupied hand, he grabbed Japheth under his arm with a crushing grip, lifted him halfway off the ground, and began effortlessly dragging Japheth towards Lux.

Japheth panicked. Aside from being incapacitated, if he were to use the fulgur spell he would be right next to Lux. If the spell had the same effect as the stories in the book, he would surely be killed along with Vesuvius.

Vesuvius began speaking as they neared Lux. "You are more

resourceful I than I had given you credit for. Pretending to be weaker than you were was an intelligent way to get me to relax and be a little careless. If your aim had been better with your knife, I would be lying on the ground right now. It's fortunate for me that it was not.

"Trying to bring mankind under subjection is sometimes a dirty and unpleasant business, but every so often it can be enjoyable. This is one of those times. I will kill you now, and I will take your sword. Eventually, I will be unstoppable once I learn how to use it. Because you are so fond of it, I think it fitting that I use it to end your miserable life. I will kill you with your own weapon, no magic needed."

They neared Lux, but Japheth was still paralyzed and couldn't speak to cast any spell. Vesuvius dropped him on the ground with his back to Lux.

"Turn and look at your sword, admire it one last time," Vesuvius mocked.

Japheth tried to roll, but the grip that Vesuvius' spell had on him was too tight and he couldn't move at all.

Vesuvius noticed this and he let his fingers out ever so slightly to lessen the effect of the spell enough for Japheth to turn. That was the break that he needed.

Japheth rolled over so he could see Lux. He had made up his mind to use the fulgur spell at the cost of his own life. He reasoned that if Vesuvius was defeated it would be a great blessing to the entire land, and more importantly to him, his family.

Vesuvius allowed him to gaze upon it for a few moments, then he removed it from the ground and raised it over his head to strike Japheth. As the sword reached its pinnacle, Japheth yelled out, "Fulgur!"

He was looking Vesuvius in the eyes as he did. He noticed the fear of realization in Vesuvius the instant before there was a blinding flash and the deafening crack of thunder.

Eli heard the crash of thunder and turned back to look at where he had come from. He could see smoke rising from what he knew was the little clearing where Vesuvius had been. He reversed course and started back to find his son. Doubts went through his mind. Why had he trusted that Japheth could defeat Vesuvius? How could he have left him? He was still contemplating his mistake when he reached the small clearing.

There at the edge of the clearing where Japheth had entered, lay his son face down with Lux next to his body, and the charred cloak of Vesuvius.

CHAPTER 17

Japheth woke up in bed. His entire body ached. As he looked himself over, he could see that he was bruised over a good portion of his body. His stirring alerted his mother.

Abigail came into the room. She knelt by her son, and smiling asked, "How do you feel?"

"About like I look," he answered.

"Well, at least you're still with us. It is a miracle that you survived."

"Survived what?" Japheth asked. His mind was still clouded, and he couldn't remember how he had got beaten up so badly.

Abigail looked at him quizzically. "Your battle with Vesuvius of course."

His mother's words brought an instantaneous flood of memories and it was then clear to him what had happened.

"I should be dead," Japheth said. "I was planning to use the fulgur spell against him, but when I did, I was so close I thought there was no way that I would survive."

"Well, whatever happened you have rid us of Vesuvius."

"How can that be?" Japheth inquired. "I was right next to him when the lightning came. It is impossible for it to have killed him and not me."

"Your father is the one that found you. He came upon you laying on the ground with Lux next to you. All that was left of Vesuvius was his burnt cloak. The grass and trees around you had been scorched," his mother answered.

Japheth sat in bewilderment, not knowing what to think.

"Maybe it's like when your body gets quickened by Lux," his mother thought out loud.

"What do you mean?" Japheth asked.

"It's not a spell that you cast or anything that you do. Lux just kind of makes it happen. Maybe it protected you from the lightning," Abigail offered.

"That's not how it's worked in the past," Japheth countered. "What does grandmother think?"

Abigail's eyes began to water, and a tear rolled down her cheek, "Japheth," she said tenderly, "she has passed on."

Japheth's heart sank. "What? How?" he asked.

His mother answered, "When Vesuvius came, she stalled him so your father could get close enough for a shot. She was successful, but Vesuvius used some type of spell against her that broke her whole body up. She had multiple broken bones and was bleeding on the inside.

"After he cast it, she fell from the rooftop she was on. I ran to her side and that's when the fire from the dragon began to fall. I used the clipeum spell to shield us from it. I drug her away from the wall. Then the other side of town began to catch fire. We evacuated into the woods.

"She struggled to stay alive for a day before she passed. I thought you would like to know that she did live long enough to know that you defeated Vesuvius. She said that her sacrifice was worth it if he was defeated.

"She also wanted me to tell you not to be sad. Once the sword is passed on, the one that used to wield it has little time left in life. It is just the natural order of things."

Tears were falling from Japheth's eyes. Through his training with her, he had developed a strong connection with Tabitha, and he had become even closer to her than before.

"How long have I been unconscious?" he asked.

"Almost three days," Eli said as he limped into the room. He was still feeling the effects of his encounter with Vesuvius, and healing came very slowly. Eli knelt at his son's side and embraced him in a hug. "Son, I am so proud of you. You have shown tremendous courage and wisdom in beating Vesuvius. After I encountered him, all my instincts told me to run, but you pressed forward and did what had to be done. You have secured freedom for all of us, and the entire community is extremely thankful."

"I think that's different," Japheth replied. "I had Lux to help me."

"Yes you did, but it still took resolve to do what you did."

———— ◆ ————

Japheth stayed in bed and ate the rest of the day. He was given all the food and water that he wanted so he could begin to get this strength back. He recounted to his family how he had defeated Vesuvius. Though his body ached, relief filled his mind. The threat was gone, and they could begin rebuilding their lives now. He was deeply saddened at the loss of his grandmother, but he knew that she would have gladly given her life to defend her family.

Japheth woke the next day and gingerly moved about the house. He was feeling much better around noon and he decided to go for a walk around the town.

He saw men, women, and children working to rebuild the town. The attack from the dragons had burned most of Licentia. There were only a handful of houses that were saved, and sparse remnants of the wall remained.

As he moved about the town, he was heartily greeted by everyone who recognized him, which was most everyone. It was obvious that there was a deep feeling of gratitude for what their family had done for the town.

In his movements around town, he met Thaddeus who flashed him a glowing smile. "Well, how is our hero feeling today?"

"I'll be fine eventually if you're talking about me, but again I'm no hero," Japheth replied.

"Well you can't tell that to these people, they know better," Thaddeus retorted. "They witnessed firsthand what you and your family have done for them, and in their eyes, you are all heroes.

Everyone has lost much, but without you, there would have been no victory against Vesuvius."

"I don't know," Japheth said, "I have seen you fight, and I think you would have found some way to beat him."

"You're probably right, but I don't want steal your glory," Thaddeus replied as he smiled and winked at Japheth.

His countenance turned more somber. "I'm sorry about your grandmother. She was a wonderful lady and a tremendous teacher. I thoroughly enjoyed my time with her. I not only learned about magic, which I still can't do, but I also learned a lot about how to be a teacher and a good person. She always put the needs of others above her own. She will be missed by more than your family."

"Thanks Thaddeus, I think she was a pretty impressive person too," Japheth replied. He didn't try to say more as his emotions were threatening to surface.

Japheth made his way back to the house he was staying in and saw his aunt Deborah sitting with her hands in a bucket of water.

"Are you going to be alright?" he asked.

"Yes, of course, I'll be fine. It's just something I will have to learn to live with."

"How long can you go without it burning?"

"It depends," she replied. "If I soak them in water and get them cooled down, I can go about an hour until they get uncomfortably hot. When mother would do the conglacior spell I was okay for a few hours, but I haven't let anyone else try it. I'm afraid they'll give me frostbite," she said with a forced smile.

"Isn't there anything we can do? Some kind of spell or potion or something?" he asked.

"Not that I know of, Abigail has gone through the book, but there doesn't seem to be anything else we can do. But Japheth, let me tell you that I would do it again, and I would lose mother again to attain the victory we have. Now we have a chance to move on with life."

Japheth decided to ask the question that had been on his mind for a while. "Aren't you angry at James?"

Deborah thought for a second, then replied. "I was a little at first, but considering what he had lost, and what he thought he had lost, I guess I can understand why he would have taken Lux. I have found that we gain a lot of compassion if we put ourselves in other people's shoes. If he hadn't, maybe things wouldn't have turned out as they did, maybe it ended up being a good thing."

"I guess you're right, I had never thought about it like that."

Japheth sat at the family book and began going over it again. He had read through it many times but this time he searched carefully for anything that may contain any type of hint or implication of something that could work for his aunt Deborah. He found nothing.

Abigail walked into the room.

"Mother, grandmother had talked of another book. A book that contained the old language, that was a kind of key to understanding how our spells and that language were related. Do you think that book would have something in it to help aunt Deborah?"

Abigail thought for a moment. "I don't know, I guess it could. Why do you ask?"

"I think I would like to try to find it," he replied.

"Oh absolutely not," she responded. "It is much too dangerous to go into Ferox. The books existence is only a legend. It may not even exist, it may never have existed. It is not prudent to take that much of a risk for something that is most likely a fable."

Japheth did not like his mother's response. "Even so mother, I would like to try. Aunt Deborah is going to suffer her entire life."

"That is true, but it is a decision that she made on her own, and if it came down to it, she would make the same decision again. Go ask her."

"She already told me as much. But if it hadn't been for her, this entire town, and all of us would have been burned and Vesuvius would still be trying to make slaves of everyone. I think we owe it to her," he protested.

"I understand that you are grateful and want to help, but my answer is, and will always be no," she countered. "Besides we may be able to determine a way to bring her relief through a potion or something else."

Japheth didn't like his mother's decision, but he decided not to push the issue further.

That night Japheth's sleep was troubled. He dreamed that Vesuvius was attacking the town. He saw scores of soldiers coming over the wall. He saw Vesuvius kill his grandmother. He saw his aunt Deborah confront him and run away screaming with her hands on fire. Then Vesuvius turned his attention to Japheth, but when he tried to challenge him his mind was blank, and he was totally helpless. He had Lux, but it wouldn't work for him. He awoke in a sweat with the image of Licentia being attacked by Vesuvius' dragons and burning to the ground.

CHAPTER 18

Japheth awoke extremely unsettled by his dream. He wanted to search for the ancient book to help his aunt Deborah, but he also wondered if the day would ever come that the knowledge in their family book would not be enough. It nearly hadn't been to defeat Vesuvius.

Japheth sat on the front porch of the house and contemplated his dream as he watched the sun come up.

Eli was the next person awake, and he gingerly made his way outside to sit beside his son. Eli had still not recovered from his encounter with Vesuvius.

Japheth followed the same line of reasoning about why he wanted to go look for the ancient book with his father. Then he added in his dream, and how uncomfortable it made him.

"Son, it was only a dream," Eli said. "It was just you reliving the traumatic events of the last few days. I understand you want to help your aunt Deborah. After all, if it weren't for her stubbornness in preparing the dragonsbane things could have turned out much differently. Your mother talked with me about your desire last night, and I think she is right. The book may not even exist, and the quest will be treacherous. I may be somewhat inclined to disagree with her if I could go with you, but my injuries are not healing and I'm afraid I would only be a hindrance to you if you did try to get through Ferox."

"What if I could find another to go in your stead?" Japheth asked eagerly.

"I'm not sure I trust anyone enough to protect my son."

After breakfast, Japheth set out to find Thaddeus. If there was anyone in the community that Eli trusted, it was Thaddeus. As he was making his way around Licentia he came across another whom he might ask to go with him, James. At first, Japheth though it to be a foolish notion. James had stolen from him and betrayed the entire town, he also had a son to look after. Something kept nagging at him to approach James with the idea, hesitantly he did so.

"James," he called out, "can I speak with you a few moments?"

James was melancholy in his appearance and demeanor, but he stopped to talk with Japheth.

Japheth explained his idea to James and added, "I know you have your son to take care of, but I was hoping that you would go with me."

James' eyes began to water slightly. "My son died. Our house was burned down in the dragons attack. My son was inside asleep because he had taken ill. The house burned so quickly that I think the smoke may have choked him before he had even woken up."

"I'm sorry," Japheth replied. "I didn't know."

"It's alright, in some ways I feel like it is repayment for my treachery against this town and its people," he said.

Japheth didn't know how to console James, he was just a young man and not experienced enough in life to say anything insightful, so he simply said what he thought was best. "I don't think it's fair that a parent should bury their child, but I guess life happens differently for each of us to teach us the lessons that we need to learn."

James thought for a few moments about Japheth's words. They seemed to carry a lot of truthfulness in them. "I will go with you if you can get your parents to agree. I will not be party to you defying your father and mother. But I don't think they would find a thief to be a very suitable traveling companion for their son."

Japheth responded to James' derogatory comments about himself. "My mother may have a harder time than my father. He told me that he recognized you from the great battle because you fought so hard and fearlessly. He has often told me when I err, one mistake won't define you, but the way that you learn and move on from it might. Thank you for agreeing to go." Japheth put out his hand, and he and James shook on the agreement, then he turned and again began to search for Thaddeus.

He found him just inside the forest cutting down a tree to use for someone's new cabin.

"Thaddeus, I have a proposition for you. It is dangerous, ill-advised, and currently against the wishes of my parents."

"I was thoroughly intrigued until I heard that last part. I respect your parents too much to help you defy them."

Japheth grinned at Thaddeus. "Well if I can get you to agree with me it might change their mind."

Japheth ran through his plan with Thaddeus and added that James had already agreed to go.

"James?" Thaddeus asked. "Why him?"

"I don't know. Probably just because he is willing to go," Japheth responded. "Do you trust him, Thaddeus?"

"I don't. There is a difference between forgiving someone and giving them another chance. It is something different to trust them to stand beside you in life.

"There is something you should know about Ferox. I have heard comparable stories from different sources. The land turns the animals against you and one another. The gist of the stories is that when riders begin into Ferox, their horses are fine at first. The further in they go, the jumpier and more fidgety they get. If pressed on, they get increasingly belligerent, and after that, they get almost adversarial with their riders. They develop disdain for them and the other horses. If the journey continues, it ends with the horses attacking their masters and each other."

"I think it best if we leave that part out," Japheth said with a hint of apprehension. "It won't help my case with my parents. Besides we can always proceed on foot."

"If you do talk your parents into it, I think we could leave James with the horses. He could probably be trusted with something like that," Thaddeus suggested.

"Will you come with me to talk to my parents?" Japheth asked.

"I haven't even agreed to go," Thaddeus replied. "I think this is something between you and them."

"Both of my parents hold you in high regard."

"I'd like to keep it that way. Trying to convince them that they should let their son go on a wild, dangerous adventure with me at his side may not be the best way to keep their respect.

"You go talk to them, and if they agree, I'll go. Otherwise, I'm going to be busy starting my new life here in Licentia."

Japheth started for home, less than hopeful that he would be able to talk his parents into letting him go look for the book that may be able to help his aunt Deborah. As he proceeded through town, he made up his mind that if they would not allow him to go, he would make preparations and go anyway, alone if he had to.

He was genuinely concerned about his aunt, but part of him was curious about what other secrets the book could hold. If another threat presented itself, he may need to be more knowledgeable than he currently was to protect his family, and he felt like the book could be the key to gaining that knowledge.

That evening after they had eaten their meal, he sat down with his parents to tell them he had recruited Thaddeus and James to go with him. It did not go over as well as he had hoped.

"Japheth, I've already told you it is not worth the risk," Abigail said. "It is far too dangerous."

Japheth looked at his father, pleading to him with his stare. Eli did not answer immediately. Abigail noticed his silence.

"I hope you are not seriously considering encouraging this," she said.

"I am," Eli said. "He has only the best of intentions, and it would be a great relief to your sister."

"Eli, we can't let him go. No man comes back from Ferox."

"That much is true, but no man has displayed the kind of power that Japheth seems to command either. No man in your family book, outside of Merlin, has been able to harness the power of Lux as Japheth has. Thaddeus would be with him as well, and I trust him as much as any man."

"And what about the thief?" she replied. "I suppose you trust him too?"

"Not nearly to the degree that I trust Thaddeus. James has had to make some difficult decisions and looking back on them, I'm not sure I would have chosen differently. A man will do foolish things when he is desperate.

"Having said that, I believe you are right Abigail. It is just too dangerous son. We cannot allow you to go."

Japheth did not protest. He simply went off to bed without another word.

He lay in bed making plans for what he would need to take, and how he would sneak out of town. After hours of waiting patiently in his bed for the rest of his family to fall asleep, he got up and wrote a note to his parents about where he was going. He grabbed Lux, his bow, throwing knives, some food, and his cloak. He had a cloak made of waterproofed wool that he knew would keep him warm and dry, no matter what circumstances he found himself in. Just before he left, he grabbed his pouch of dragonsbane and tied it to his belt. Then he sneaked out the door.

He made his way to the stable to get his horse. As he pushed the door open, he was greeted with a friendly, "Hello Japheth."

"Thaddeus, what are you doing here?" Japheth asked.

"Waiting for you."

"How did you know I'd be out here?"

Thaddeus answered, "Because I know what it's like to be young and determined. I could tell when you came to talk to me today that you were not going to take no for an answer. I decided that I would get ready and wait. If you showed up, I'd go with you, if you didn't, I would consider the issue dropped.

"I also went and talked to James, he is coming with us."

"Thank you, Thaddeus," Japheth said gratefully. "I was ready to go alone, but I do feel much more confident having help."

"After seeing what you could do with that sword, I'm not sure you need any help, but I think if I'm with you it might keep your parents from coming after us."

"How will they know?" Japheth asked.

"They are intelligent people Japheth, when they get up in the morning and you, I, and James are gone, they will know what happened."

The three men quietly left Licentia and headed south towards Ferox. It would take days for them to reach its borders, and if they were honest with themselves, none of them were too anxious to get there.

CHAPTER 19

The riders took a lackadaisical pace as they continued south. It had been three days since they left Licentia, and since they had not seen anyone from the town, they decided that no one was coming to stop them.

On the way, Thaddeus shared everything he knew or had heard about Ferox so they could be as prepared as possible. James was able to add a few things, but nothing substantiated, he had never been in or near Ferox, so all the information he had was secondhand.

Japheth was able to add some information he had learned from his grandmother before she died. Although she had never been there, it seemed like her information was reliable.

Japheth also told the story of the book, as much as he had been told by his grandmother, to Thaddeus and James. In his time studying with her, she had told him all she had learned about it. There was a time before Merlin, when wizards were becoming increasingly powerful, which caused concern among those that were not magical.

There was a book that contained a long-forgotten language holding the key to their spells. The keeper of the book, Godun, had learned of a plot to steal the book and destroy it for the good of mankind by his king. Not wanting that to happen he took the book from the castle and left for Ferox. All that was within the castle was considered to be the property of the king. He knew that he would now be viewed as a thief and would not be allowed to return unpunished. After he left, he was pursued by the king's men. He evaded them for a while, but there was a confrontation and he killed a large portion of the king's army. Having stolen from the king, and now crippling his army he would not be shown any mercy if he returned, so he unselfishly left his old life behind, never to see his family again.

In the center of Ferox, there is a mountain which stands taller than the rest that is especially inhospitable. It is visible from the edges of Ferox and is known simply as Black Mountain. It gets its name from its composition of basalt and obsidian. Large, jagged sections of granite jut out from the mountain. Minor eruptions occur randomly from the base to the peak, releasing fresh flows of lava that ooze down the sides in rivers of molten rock. Near the summit is a concealed cave. The book was taken there and left. Godun left Ferox to draw the attention of his king away from there so they wouldn't find the book. He left clues and rumors among the wizards of the time so that the location of the book would not be forgotten, with the hopes that one day someone would find it, and hopefully, preserve it.

It was discussed among them what they should do with the horses, as they had decided it would not be safe to ride them through Ferox. They concluded that when they had gone as far as they were comfortable, James would stay with them, and Thaddeus and Japheth would continue on foot.

They traveled a few more days, and at evening they came to what was considered the borders of Ferox. It was not an abrupt change, but one of the distinct features of Ferox was the earth moan. A constant, low pitched moan seemed to emanate from the ground. It sounded like a tree when it is pushed back and forth by the wind. It was not loud, but the unrelenting noise had an eerie feel to it.

They decided to ride a bit further before stopping to make camp. A few somewhat dark clouds had moved in and masked the sun, giving the surrounding terrain a more foreboding look. As they were riding through a small group of trees, a streak of lightning came from nowhere and struck the tree next to them. A branch broke from the tree and as it fell, it struck Thaddeus across the body and knocked him from his horse to the ground.

James and Japheth regained control of their horses and dismounted to help Thaddeus. His horse had run off and he was sitting on the ground holding his arm.

"I think it's broken," Thaddeus said as he looked and James and Japheth.

"Can you go on?" James asked.

"I think I will be alright," Thaddeus replied, grimacing.

Japheth voiced his concern, "Thaddeus, Ferox is no place to go if you don't feel entirely yourself. Strong, healthy men go in, but don't come back out."

"I don't need to be myself, I just need to stay close to you. I have perfect trust in you and that sword."

James interrupted, "Thaddeus, Japheth is right, you should stay with the horses and I will go with him to find the book."

Thaddeus knew that he would be more of a hindrance than a help to Japheth if he accompanied him. Yet he did not fully trust James to look after Japheth.

Looking at James he said, "I still have some reservations about your resolve to protect Japheth. I think you have good intentions, but when a situation tests your mettle, how will you respond?"

James paused before answering, "I can understand why you wouldn't trust me, and if I were in your place, I wouldn't trust me either. I made a major mistake and it nearly cost everyone I know their lives.

"However, when Eli and his family did not expose me for the traitorous act I made against my community, I made him a promise, a promise that I would look after his family as I would my own in an effort to repay the kindness and forgiveness that their family extended to me.

"Despite my poor choice in the past, I fully intend to keep that promise. I know that may not mean much to you, but it does to me. I give you my word that I will do all that is within my power to keep Japheth safe, at any cost to myself."

Thaddeus could see sincerity in James' demeanor. "I believe you," he said. As he smiled, he continued, "Now of course when we return with the book, I expect both of you to tell everyone how difficult it was to convince me to stay behind, even with my broken arm. I have somewhat of a reputation to keep up in Licentia."

James and Japheth agreed, returning his smile.

They made camp that night and ran through their revised plans to successfully get into Ferox, find the book, and get back out.

It was decided that Japheth would be the key to all of them surviving, so he would not be required to take a turn at watch that night. James would take first watch, but Thaddeus would remain awake through the bulk of the night so James could be as refreshed as possible for the next day's journey.

Surprisingly, Japheth slept well through the uneventful night.

At daybreak, as the three men ate their breakfast of dried fruit and meat there was little conversation. Black Mountain could be seen in the distance, so losing sight of their destination should not be a problem, how they were going to get there would be.

Thaddeus rehearsed their most basic plan just to make sure they were all in agreeance. "Now remember, I'll stay here for ten days. If you are longer than that I will assume that the worst has happened. I will leave one horse here just in case you make it back after I have left. You will travel in a straight line from here to Black Mountain. If you must change course, move to the east. That way when I come back with more men, we will know what direction to look for you. Try to mark your route with broken branches so we can tell if we are on your trail.

"I think we can forget about you signaling me with a bonfire from the top of Black Mountain if you find the book. Last night as I watched there were enough eruptions around the mountain that I don't think I could distinguish them from a fire."

Japheth acknowledged his words. "Okay Thaddeus. Don't worry about us, we will be fine. Just make sure the horses are taken care of and try to find yours if you can. It would be a much better ride home if we each had our own horse."

"I should have enough time to find him," Thaddeus said as he looked at James and Japheth, "Godspeed."

Japheth and James started for Black Mountain.

The two men talked periodically as they walked. They kept their voices low. Nothing seemed out of the ordinary yet, but with all the things they had heard about Ferox they thought it best to stay alert and attentive to any dangers that might be present. When they began their journey, the forest had been somewhat sparse, but the further they walked, the thicker the trees became. The wind also began to pick up, making a constant rustling sound as it passed through the forest.

Not long after noon, they could make out what looked like a clearing in front of them. When they emerged from the trees, they could see a lush, green field ahead. It appeared to sprawl out all the way to Black Mountain.

"This is a lucky break," Japheth said. "I didn't think we'd find something like this in Ferox. I had heard it was nothing but difficult terrain. This almost looks inviting."

"You're right, it does look quite harmless, but we shouldn't get our hopes up, or let our guard down. I'm sure there is more to this than it seems," James returned.

"Relax James," Japheth replied. "Don't be so pessimistic."

Japheth began walking across the green field in front of them. He hadn't walked very far when he suddenly stopped.

"Ow!" he exclaimed. He lifted his boot to see a huge thorny mass sticking through the bottom of his boot and into his foot. He pulled it from his boot and examined it.

James walked up next to him and looked at the thorn as well. "It's in the shape of a caltrop."

"What is that?" Japheth asked.

"A caltrop is a spiked metal device in a shape that leaves at least one spike pointing upwards regardless of how it is setting on the ground. The king's army sometimes uses them.

"Look, these vines that cover this field grow them."

As Japheth looked out over the open field, he could see hundreds, maybe thousands of the thorns covering the ground.

James continued, "I don't think we are getting to Black Mountain this way. We'll have to go around."

"Maybe," Japheth replied. "Let me try something first."

Japheth removed Lux, held out his hand, and cast the ignis spell. A river of fire shot from his hand and engulfed the green, sprawling plants in front of him, they almost seemed to recoil from the heat. Once the fire had died out, they looked over the field again.

While the fire had burned the plants, it left the thorns unscathed. They were easy to see but too thick to walk through.

"I guess you are right. It would take us way too long to reach Black Mountain this way," Japheth conceded. "We would have to burn them, and then move them out of the way to get through here. I guess we had better start moving east."

James agreed and the pair walked back to the trees and began following the tree line east, hacking off branches to mark their trail as they went.

CHAPTER 20

The plants that produced the caltrop thorns seemed to need lots of sunlight to grow. As long as they stayed inside the forest where it was shady there were no thorns. If they ventured too far out of the trees, they would step on one now and then.

The traveling was much easier, and quicker, outside of the trees, but the thorns made it more practical to travel inside the forest.

They had been walking for a couple of hours when they got the distinct feeling that they were being watched. They both sensed it, and they began moving more cautiously to better observe the area around them. Japheth drew Lux to be ready if he needed it.

Suddenly Japheth heard a slight rustling to his right. He turned his head just in time to see a monstrous spider beginning its leap towards them.

He yelled, clipeum just quickly enough for the spider to crash into the shield it produced.

Japheth faced the stunned spider and brought his sword down, cutting it in two.

He heard James yell and turned to see him fending off another of the beastly spiders. Just as James ran his sword through its body, Japheth could see another leaping from a tree towards James. He reached out his hand and yelled, "Inpulsa!" A shock left his hand and hit the spider in midair. The spider's legs curled up underneath it as it died instantly. Its trajectory was true, and its body slammed into James, knocking him down.

Japheth could now see many more spiders working their way towards them from all sides. He quickly made his way over to James, who had risen. He held out his hand and cast the ignis spell.

He moved his hand from right to left across his body and continued in a circle until he had created a large ring of fire around them.

The fire caused some of the spiders to retreat, but a few of the others began jumping over the flames trying to get to the two men. James cut and slashed with his sword as the spiders came within reach. Japheth held Lux and used the inpulsa spell to kill them mid-jump. The assault began to diminish, and as it did Japheth used the time to cast the ignis spell again, this time creating a ring of fire out farther from them.

His spell was successful as some of the spiders caught fire and began running through the forest, lighting some of the underbrush aflame as they went. Just as quickly as it had begun, the attack was over.

Japheth looked over at James and said, "It's almost like they were working together."

"Yes, I thought the same thing. I have never seen or even heard of anything like this. Just their sheer size is alarming, but their intelligence, if they were working together, makes them absolutely terrifying."

They stopped to examine a few of the dead spiders. As far as they could tell they were just like hundreds of spiders they had seen all their lives, just much, much larger.

They decided to move on quickly. They did not want to see if the commotion would attract the attention of anything else that may be close.

As evening was approaching, they noticed a change in the landscape around them. The ground under their feet was getting damper, finally getting to the point where water would ooze out from under their boots as they walked.

The damp conditions were not favorable for the caltrop thorns, and eventually, there were no more to be found, which made travel outside of the forest more feasible. Once they had gotten to the point that they thought they could travel towards Black Mountain again they made sure to cut off multiple branches to mark their trail.

As they continued, the damp ground gave way to a mature swamp. The dark water was stagnant and had a stench to it. The water got deeper, little by little as they walked. As the deepening water reached mid-calf it slowed them more and more and became more cumbersome to travel in.

Japheth was in the lead and he noticed an almost imperceptible ripple in the water ahead, much like the ripple a fish makes as it swims through a calm pond, or lake. He took notice and became more cautious as they moved.

After a few more minutes of travel he saw it again, only this time it was more pronounced, and it looked as if there were more than one ripple. He stopped.

"What's wrong?" James asked.

"I think there may be something in the water," Japheth answered.

"I'm sure there is," James replied.

"No, not just something, but something to be wary of. I have noticed it a couple of times, and with the depth of the water I think we should be leery of whatever it is."

Japheth reached out his hand and used the calor spell. This spell was most commonly used by his family to warm up bowls of pottage or soup. He figured that with the added power of Lux, he could warm the swamp water in his vicinity to a degree that whatever was in the water would get uncomfortable enough to move.

A few moments passed with no results. He and James could slowly feel the water warming. As it began to get slightly uncomfortable, dozens of small ripples, some only a few feet away, began moving quickly away from them.

This result alarmed both James and Japheth. Continuing to hold out his hand to warm the water Japheth turned to James and said, "I think we should try to find some semi-solid ground. I'm not comfortable walking in this water anymore."

"Agreed."

Japheth continued in front, heating the water as they walked. The ripples continued moving away from the heat a fair distance in front of them, but the uncomfortable heat of the water they were walking in was beginning to wear on both of them. The sun was beginning to set, and they needed to find somewhere that they could make camp for the night.

James spotted what appeared to be an island not too far in the distance, and they made their way toward it. The ground that protruded from the swamp was not a large area, but just being able to get out of the water was a great relief. There were a few small trees on the island, but no dry wood with which to build a fire to dry themselves.

Japheth and James gathered what wet wood there was, and Japheth used the ignis spell to ignite the wet, rotting wood. They believed they were about halfway to Black Mountain, maybe even a little closer.

As the sun set, the temperature dropped much more than it should have. Soon they were able to see their breath and before they had finished eating, the top of the swamp water had begun to freeze.

They knew that if the temperature continued to drop, they would need every bit of wood they could find to keep from freezing. They were somewhat apprehensive because a fire would be sure to attract whatever was lurking about at night.

Japheth took the first watch. He noticed that the temperature had stopped dropping as quickly as it had when the sun went down. He sat with his knees pulled to his chest so his cloak could cover his body and almost keep him warm.

Japheth looked out towards Black Mountain. He could see multiple areas were lava came to the surface and ran down the mountain. Great clouds of steam rose from the lava flows.

Ferox was surprisingly quiet at night. The pessimist in Japheth had thought that, as savage as it was during the day, that the nighttime would be even worse. He sat through half of the night, with Lux ready in his hand, but he did not see anything or hear a sound. Other than the ever-present earth moan, there was nothing. He missed the sounds the crickets and frogs would make in the evenings. He longed to hear something other than the low, constant groan of the earth. By the end of his watch, the fire had managed to dry his clothes, and his boots were nearly dry as well.

He woke James to switch watches. Japheth lay with his cloak wrapped around him, his back to the fire and drifted off into a light, restless sleep.

The moon had made its way from behind the clouds and was nearly full. The light was a welcomed sight to James and it moderately eased his fears. He had not slept well. The cold and his anxiety about what may be prowling in the darkness did not allow him to get much rest.

The bulk of the night was uneventful for James as well. Just as he could make out the faintest signs of light in the east, he heard a noise off to his right. It was just a slight rustling, but it panicked him. He rose slowly, drew his sword, and moved towards the sound. His movements woke Japheth who was up and ready in an instant.

James put a finger to his mouth, indicating to Japheth to be quiet, and pointed in the direction of the sound. As the two walked towards the bank of the little island in the swamp, they noticed nothing.

Out of nowhere a long tentacle, about the thickness of a man's forearm, shot out from under the ice and wrapped around Japheth, pinning both arms to his side before either of the men could react. Japheth could feel the spikes on it bite through his skin. James brought his sword down on the feeler, nearly cutting it in two. It released its grip on Japheth and began drawing quickly back into the water. Japheth fell to the ground as it unwrapped from around him.

Before it was submerged two more appendages shot out from the icy water. One headed towards Japheth and the other towards James. James was able to lift his arm wielding his sword up, before the tentacle wrapped around him. Japheth had sat up and again the tentacle wrapped completely around his body.

In the instant the decision had to be made, James remembered his promise to Eli, to protect his family as his own, and he brought his sword down on the tentacle constricting Japheth. His blow severed the end of the feeler.

As he raised his arm to strike again, he was jerked violently off his feet dropping his sword.

Japheth watched as he disappeared under the water, the wave and breaking ice created by his body quickly drifted from his sight.

Japheth sat alone, bleeding, and stunned by what had just happened. For the first time since he left Licentia, he felt like he would fail. He looked out over the frozen water of the marsh, terrified by what lies within its waters. He realized that if James had not acted so swiftly and selflessly it would have been him being dragged to his death. He was petrified at the thought of getting back into the water, whether it was to try to get to Black Mountain, or to try to get back home.

He sat for a few moments, wanting to cry, wanting to scream, wanting to hide. He knew none of those things would help him. Ferox was a far more terrible place than he had imagined from the stories.

Then an idea crossed his mind. If the ice was thick enough to walk on perhaps, he could get across the swamp before it thawed. He forced himself to his feet, faced Black Mountain, and began walking out onto the ice.

CHAPTER 21

After his first few steps, he knew his idea wouldn't work. He broke through the fragile ice with each step. He nervously hurried back out of the water, paranoid of what might wait for him beneath its surface.

He gripped Lux desperately, searching his mind for a solution. Then he remembered the messengers, and how they had caused an oak tree to freeze solid. He stepped to the edge of the island and said, "Conglacior." Immediately the putrid water became solid. He stepped out on it and it felt as firm as earth beneath his feet. He began walking.

After about a hundred feet the ice became less stable and he repeated the conglacior spell. Once more the water instantly froze solid and he continued. He moved this way nervously for hours, skittishly making his way towards Black Mountain.

The sun had risen, and the uneasiness caused by limited sight in the darkness slowly left him. As he walked, he noticed that some of the creatures in the water had gotten caught in the ice as it froze. The water was dark, and it made seeing very far into the ice nearly impossible, but every now and again he would see something caught in the ice.

He came upon what looked to him to be the top of a turtle shell, as big as a wagon wheel, protruding from the ice, its black shell littered with twisted spikes. Then he saw what he could only describe as a freakishly large fish. Its eyes frozen open seemed to glare at him with malice. Instead of scales, it appeared to be covered with thick plating. Its teeth looked jagged and sharp, as if they could clean the meat off a man's bones with little effort.

As he continued freezing and crossing the swamp there was a great thrashing up ahead of him. As he neared, he could see that it was an enormous snake. How long it was he could not tell. It had been partially frozen in the ice, and it struggled to free itself. The snake was dark, like the swamp water, a perfect camouflage for its environment. As he neared, the snake's urgency increased, and it struggled more wildly. Japheth, not wanting any kind of confrontation, cast the inpulsa spell. The shock hit the massive serpent, and it lay still in the ice.

Around midday, he reached the end of the swamp where it met the base of Black Mountain. He began walking up the slope. The mountain was not made of soil as he had expected. It was composed of loose shards of obsidian, or dark flint. Nothing grew on its foreboding slopes, they were completely devoid of any vegetation. He struggled to get away from the frightening swamp, and whatever was lurking beneath its waters.

Walking was a struggle. His boots sank into the hard, loose fragments that made up the mountain. It seemed like for every step he took he slid back half the distance. Several time he faltered and set his hand down to right himself. Each time he would receive small cuts on his hand from the fractured rock and glass. When he had gotten enough separation between him and the marsh, he sat.

He sat for a long while, reliving the events of the past day in a state of shock. He wondered how he could ever make it back home, wondering what type of beast would bring him down. Would it be a quick and painless death, or would he suffer? Would it be something he had already seen, or would it be some new horror yet undiscovered? What would become of Thaddeus and those that came with him to search? Surely they would come, and he knew they would all die.

His mind continued dwelling on the worst that could happen in this place, and as it did, he felt deeper and deeper despair.

Then he began reflecting on the time he had spent with his grandmother. How she was always so happy and positive about everything life threw at her. He knew she would not have wanted him to come searching for the book, for she understood the dangers of Ferox far better than he could have. He longed to be back home with her, learning from her wise counsel.

He longed to be with his parents and siblings, working on the farm and hunting in the forest. He wanted his simple life back. The one he had before he had accepted Lux, when he only saw benefits of having the sword, ignorant of the responsibilities that came with it.

He resolved in his mind to press on, no matter how dismal his situation seemed. He was very doubtful that, if he did indeed find the book, he could make it back home with it. Still, if he was going to die, he would face that death bravely.

He pulled a piece of cheese and some dried meat from his sack, quickly ate, and began his lonely hike up the mountain.

The rest of the day was a blur. The slow progress allowed his mind to wander. He was suspicious of every perceived movement, most of which were only in his mind. He felt vulnerable hiking up the mountain. There wasn't cover of any kind. Anyone, or anything, on that mountain would be able to see him coming from a long way off. Conversely, with there being nowhere to hid, nothing could conceal itself from him either.

From a distance the lava flows looked close together, but now that he was on the mountain, there was a lot of space between them in which to climb. He hoped he could walk on the large gran-ite protrusions to get out of the loose fragments of the mountain, but climbing them would be slower, and more dangerous than sim-ply struggling up the mountain.

As the day grew short, Japheth neared the peak. The slope be-came steeper, but the ground became firmer under his feet. He questioned how long it would take him to find the cave, if he could find it at all.

He couldn't be sure which had tired him more. Walking in the deep water of the swamp, or the loose ground of the mountain. Both had taken their toll, and his muscles ached.

He stopped to rest, and as he leaned on his sword, he could see that not far up the hill, the ground leveled off somewhat. He reasoned that it would be a good place to stop for the night.

Just as he was about to begin climbing again, a faint movement above him caught his eye. He stood motionless and stared at the ground above him. He felt uneasy like he knew something was there, but he could not see anything.

As he continued scanning the terrain his eyes fixed on something that almost looked familiar. The moment that he realized what it was it began to move. What he saw was the eye of a dragon.

As the beast rose it uncovered itself. It had burrowed itself almost completely in the loose, dark, gravel-like soil of the mountain.

When it reached full height Japheth could see that it was much larger than the other dragons he had seen. He also noticed something that made it different from the other dragons, it had no wings. It slowly made its way down the slope, never lifting its gaze from Japheth.

Japheth steadied his mind. He knew if the dragon tried using fire that he could successfully defend himself and use it against the dragon. If it simply came after him, he had many spells at his disposal.

Not wanting to wait to see what the dragon would try, Japheth cast the inpulsa spell. A shock leapt from his hand and encompassed the dragon. Slightly stunned, the dragon roared and prepared to breathe fire. When it did Japheth exclaimed, "Captis!"

As before the fire spiraled into Lux. Next, Japheth yelled, "Exsolvo!" The fire that was moments before being discharged by the dragon now surged towards it. As the fire enveloped the dragon Japheth's heart sank.

The dragon stood there, unharmed by the fire. Japheth panicked. As the dragon rushed down towards him, aflame, all he could think to do was use the clipeum spell. As he did the nearly invisible shield materialized before him. The dragon crashed into it, and fell dazed, onto its side. The impact caused Japheth to stumble down the hill.

From above the dragon's position Japheth heard a man yell, "Grunge, cease!"

Japheth looked and saw him coming quickly down the mountain. The dragon got to its feet, and as obediently as any trained dog, sat and waited for its master, fire still covered its body.

Japheth stood alert and ready.

The man made his way down to the dragon. He looked to be about his father's age. He raised his hand and muttered a few words. The fire that just a few moments before was burning viciously, extinguished in an instant. The man reached out and stroked the dragons massive head before turning to look at Japheth.

"We don't get many visitors here," he said. The tone of his voice was not threatening, nor was it welcoming.

"You have my respect simply because you stand before me. Getting through Ferox alive is a monumental feat. It has been over fifty years since I have seen another living man here. Tell me stranger, did you get here through the swamp, desert, forest, or through the thorns?"

Japheth responded confidently, "I came through the swamp."

"That is most impressive. Of all the visitors I have had through the years you are the first to make it through the swamp. Most come through the desert, no one has yet to make it through the thorns."

Japheth's curiosity about the dragon not burning was at the forefront of his mind, he could not hold his question back, "How is it that this dragon did not burn?"

The man turned and looked back at the dragon before answering. "Every so often a dragon is born that is immune to the effects of fire, even the intense fire of another dragon. It is easy to tell which dragons have this particular trait, they have no wings.

"Even without wings, dragons make wonderful guardians. Their high level of intelligence makes them more predictable, and trainable than any other animal. Grunge here is one of the oldest dragons alive, he and I have been companions for many hundreds of years."

The man turned back to Japheth. "Now you must tell me how it is that you were able to absorb his fire and launch it back at him."

Japheth was leery about telling him how it was done, but not being able to think of some other believable explanation he told the truth. "It's the sword."

The man looked quizzically at Japheth and asked, "What do you mean? I trust you must be a powerful wizard, as am I, but even with my lifetimes of experience I cannot do what I have just witnessed, you must explain it to me."

"This sword has been passed down in my family for generations. It can magnify the power of whoever it chooses to wield it," Japheth explained, he didn't want to go into any more detail than necessary.

The man continued, "Tell me, how did your family come to possess such a magnificent weapon?"

"It was forged by an early ancestor of mine," Japheth answered, hesitant to elaborate.

"And who was that ancestor?"

Japheth paused for a few brief moments before answering, "Merlin."

A smile crossed the man's face. "The Merlin?"

Japheth answered in the affirmative, "Yes, The Merlin."

The man looked off into the distance as if trying to remember a long-forgotten memory. When he spoke, his words shocked Japheth. "You know, I met him once, so very many years ago. He was a brilliant wizard."

"You cannot be that old," Japheth said. "You look to be about my father's age."

"I can't give you an exact number of years, after so long you quit caring, and quit counting."

Japheth asked, "What is your name?"

"Godun," the man answered.

"You're the keeper of the book!" Japheth said excitedly, his apprehension giving way to optimism. "You saved it from being destroyed and brought it here."

"I am the keeper of many books, and many magical artifacts as well," he returned.

"I am talking about a book that contains the old language, the one that our spells are derived from," Japheth said, hoping to clarify which book he spoke of.

"Yes, I guess that would be the book that most would look for," he replied.

Japheth's excitement started to be replaced with reason. It was impossible for this to be the Godun that saved the book. "You can't be the Godun that saved the book, that was hundreds of years ago."

Godun smiled and replied, "It was hundreds of years ago, but I am the same Godun. The book contains many great things to the casual reader of it, but if one looks closely at the details and takes the time to properly contemplate them, a whole new understanding, and mountains of knowledge can be obtained from it."

Japheth looked skeptically at the man. "If you are Godun, tell me the story of how the book got here."

"Alright, I'll tell you. Many lifetimes ago there was a great battle. My king, Vortigern, had just defeated our greatest foe. As the current story is told today, they were barbarians from the north. While they were a savage people the label barbarian does not fit. They were unrelenting, and vicious, but extremely clever. They were gifted in the use of magic as well, dark magic. It was a terrible, bloody struggle. We outnumbered them significantly, and that is the only reason we were victorious."

Japheth studied the man as he spoke. He seemed to be concentrating on the memories to tell the story to the best of his knowledge. It almost seemed to Japheth as though he was actually placing himself back to the days he spoke of.

He continued, "The fact that they had so much magical power was of great concern to Vortigern. I was the kingdom wizard and I safeguarded the book." He looked at Japheth, "The same book you now seek.

"Magic was not well understood by most, and the bulk of the king's advisers wanted the book destroyed, for the safety of others they would claim. King Vortigern was also a close personal friend so I was able to dissuade him from following through on their advice.

"The opposition to wizardry kept growing to the point where he felt his hands were tied. As I was going to speak with him one evening, I overheard him speaking with his most trusted adviser. He gave the order to confiscate the book from me and destroy it. I immediately grabbed the book and fled.

"I knew this mountain would be a safe place for the book.

"In those days Ferox was not what it is today. It was wild and untamed ground, but not nearly as deadly.

"As I ran, I was confronted by a portion of the king's army. They would not allow me to continue with the book, that was unfortunate for them. During the ensuing confrontation, I killed each one of them. Not out of hate or malice but because of devotion to my craft. I could not allow nearly all the knowledge about wizardry that had been accrued over lifetimes to be destroyed.

"I came here and deposited the book. Then I left and spread rumors about where the book was. I carefully created so many ghosts for the king to pursue that he would remain forever chasing, never finding.

"I left behind a family that I never saw again. I stayed here and studied the book. As I did, the mysteries of magic were unfolded to me. I have been here ever since, venturing out every few decades to search for other books or relics that might be of interest to one such as I."

Godun looked Japheth in the eye and with all sincerity said, "I helped to make Ferox what it is today."

CHAPTER 22

"You made Ferox?" Japheth asked. "How did you make the unnatural creatures?"

"Made is not the right word," Godun answered. "Persuaded or influenced would be more accurate.

"When I first came here, Ferox was a feral land, but as I studied the book, I discovered how I could influence nature around me and help it become what I wanted it to become. Plants, animals, and even the earth itself could be manipulated. I didn't have a great need for protection, but I thought that if the land and the things on it, would protect me and the book, there was much less of a chance that I would have to fight to safeguard it.

"It turns out that, that has been true. I believe that many try, but very few make it here to Black Mountain. As the years progress the number of seekers decrease."

Japheth was satisfied with Godun's response to his question. He had no way to be certain, but he was going to assume that Godun was who he said he was. His mind quickly returned to the statement he had made that none of the men that had made it to this point had come through the thorns.

"I have another question. You said that no man had made it through the thorns. Why is that? When we came to them it looked like a fairly easy route to this mountain. If one took his time, it seems like it would be the safest route."

Godun answered, "It does seem like the safest route, but there is more to the thorns that you think. They need sunlight to grow and produce their thorns. However, if sunlight is not directly on them, they can move. The darker it is the more powerful those movements can become. I have observed travelers going through the thorns. When they stop to make camp for the night, they have condemned themselves.

"The vines wrap themselves around them and the thorns prick them. The thorns contain a venom on their tips. A dozen or so pricks will not have a noticeable effect on a man. Once someone is exposed to a hundred punctures their body starts to shut down. Out of all the ways that Ferox can kill someone, this is probably the most surprising."

Godun concluded his story and then asked Japheth, "You said 'we' came upon the thorns. Was there someone with you?"

Japheth nodded his head, "Yes, I came with a man from my town. Something in the swamp got him."

"What was it?" Godun asked.

"I don't know," Japheth answered. "It looked like a couple of large vines that shot out from beneath the ice. They got a hold of him and dragged in out into the water. What is it?"

Godun responded, "I'm not exactly sure what it is, but it is a much larger creature than you would think could conceal itself in the shallow waters of the swamp."

Japheth asked quizzically, "You don't know what it is? I thought you created it."

Godun shook his head. "I didn't create anything, I simply try to impact the way that the land, plants, and creatures develop. Without a deep and complete understanding of the book, I can't explain it to you in a way that would make sense."

"When you leave Ferox, how do you get out?" Japheth asked.

Godun replied, "I can get out any way I please, but mostly I go through the desert. The physical conditions of the desert have gotten so harsh that there are few creatures there to speak of. The land presents dangers of its own, but it is the easiest way to get in and out."

Japheth looked back out over the path he had followed to Black Mountain. Once they had gotten to the thorns had they gone west instead they would have come to the desert. He made a note of that fact to remember for when he started back for home.

Japheth turned again to Godun and spoke, "That will be good to know so that I might return home safely."

"That is true, but you may not want to go home after you have studied from the book. Once you start to learn from it, to discover its mysteries, you can easily become obsessed with searching for more knowledge. It can begin to consume your every thought and become your every desire."

Godun's words gave Japheth pause. He had never considered that there could be a detrimental effect to studying the book.

Godun looked at Japheth in a way that made him feel uneasy. "Are you ready to experience the book?"

Japheth took a few moments to steady his thoughts, then nodded slightly at Godun.

"Very well," he said, "follow me."

Japheth followed behind Godun as the pair hiked towards the level ground that he had spotted earlier. He also noticed that Grunge had nestled himself back down into the loose flint and obsidian.

The ground under his feet firmed up as they reached their destination, and Japheth looked around expecting to see a cave or dwelling of some kind. All he saw was bare rock, with large pieces of stone jutting out from the mountainside.

He continued following Godun who walked up beside one of the large fragments of stone. Where the stone met the mountain slope there was a slight opening, just big enough for a man to fit through. Godun walked inside and Japheth followed.

They had only walked a few feet when the narrow passage gave way to a large cave. As Godun walked inside he motioned with his hand and dozens of oil lamps spontaneously lit, illuminating the cave. Inside were many shelves filled with books, and potions. Around the perimeter of the cave was a bed, a fireplace, and what looked like clutter to Japheth, just a lot of random items that looked almost out of place. There was also a large table with a few chairs in the middle of the room.

Godun walked towards the bookshelves and reached for a hefty book on the bottom shelf. He pulled it out and walked to the table, setting the book down carefully. He pulled a chair out and motioned for Japheth to sit.

"Where do I start?" Japheth asked.

"At the beginning."

Japheth opened the ancient book and began reading.

At the front of the book were the potion recipes. Each one detailed the ingredients, how to properly prepare and mix them, and also spells that one could use with them to alter or enhance how each potion worked. Japheth hurried through the potions, he never had been very interested in them.

The next portion of the book contained a list of magical artifacts, some even included sketches with descriptions. Japheth slowed somewhat while looking through this part of the book. As he looked at the first few, his interest was piqued, and he wanted to see if Lux was in the book.

There were all types of enchanted items in the book. Japheth expected to see things likes staffs, wands, or weapons. While those items were included there were also more mundane items like brooms and cauldrons.

Japheth hurried through this portion of the book as well. While he did find it interesting, he was much more intrigued by what spells he hoped to find. Japheth noticed that Lux was not included in the enchanted items portion of the book.

When he finally came to the spells, Godun interrupted him. "It's nearly morning, would you like something to eat?"

Japheth looked at him confused. "What do you mean?"

"I mean you've been reading all through the night and the sun is about to come up, I thought you might be hungry."

Japheth took a moment to orient his thinking. He thought through the last little while and realized that he had gotten to Godun's in the evening. He reasoned that he must have been reading all night. As this realization came to him, he suddenly realized that his body was tired, but his mind remained active. Although it had seemed to him that he had hurried through the book, it had taken him nearly all night.

"Yes, now that you mention it, I am a little hungry."

Godun looked at him knowingly and said, "That's what I mean about becoming obsessed with the book, you can easily lose track of the time."

Godun handed him a plate with some fresh fruit and dried meat on it. Japheth looked at the fruit with confusion. He wondered how Godun would get fresh fruit here.

"Where did this fruit come from?" he asked.

Godun smiled and answered, "I grew it."

"What do you mean you grew it? Here?"

"Yes, I grew it here," Godun responded.

Japheth returned, "How did you grow it here? I haven't seen any plants since I started up the mountain."

"I can show you if you like," Godun replied.

"Yes, I would like you to show me."

Godun walked to the rows of shelves along the cave wall and retrieved a vessel with a green liquid in it. He stood before Japheth and said, "I think we'll have tomatoes at lunch." He uncorked the bottle and tilted it slightly so that only a few drops came out. They landed on the cave floor.

Godun moved his hand over the spot and muttered something very softly. In a few moments, Japheth noticed the small plant that began to sprout. He watched as it continued growing bigger, and bigger until a full-grown tomato plant, crowded with red, ripe tomatoes, stood before him. Japheth was amazed.

"How did you do that?" he asked.

"The secret lies with the book Japheth. This is just one of the many miracles that can be done with the proper knowledge."

"What spell did you use to grow that plant?" He asked.

Godun replied, "It's not so much the spell, as it is the potion. I think potions have always been overlooked. The spell is a type of enhancer, but the potion is the key."

"I didn't notice anything like that when I read about the potions," Japheth stated.

"That's because you moved through it too fast, you didn't take time to deeply study the words, each and every word. How the word was used, and why that particular word was used is often more telling that the mere definition of it."

For an instant, Japheth's mind seemed to comprehend what Godun had meant, but as quickly as the understanding had come upon him, it left. Still, he was left with a glimpse of comprehension.

Japheth responded, "I think I understand what you are saying, somewhat."

"The more time you study, the more your understanding will be opened," Godun said.

Japheth looked at the plate before him and said appreciatively, "Thank you for the food."

"Of course, you are welcome, I enjoy helping other seekers of knowledge like myself. I know you are anxious to glean what knowledge you can from the book, but might I suggest that you get some rest, at least a few hours before you continue.

"I of all people know how consuming the book can become, but if you do not allow your mind to rest you will not be as sharp as you need to be to better understand what you are reading. You would do well to rest, if only for a few hours."

Once Japheth had finished his food the truth of Godun's words were evident. He became keenly aware that he was extremely tired. Godun offered him a spot to rest in the cave and Japheth gladly accepted it. In his last moment of consciousness before drifting off to sleep he had a slight feeling of apprehension about laying down to rest.

CHAPTER 23

J apheth woke startled. His rest had not been restful. It was filled with images of the horrors he had seen in Ferox and those he had heard from Godun. The one that bothered him the most was the one of James being dragged under the ice and out of sight. His body was so tired that it forced him to remain asleep through the nightmares.

He instinctively reached for Lux only to find it was gone. He looked up, alarmed, to see Godun holding the sword. He was looking it over, studying it, like it was the most precious thing he had ever seen.

Japheth slowly stood, and Godun met his gaze.

"This is truly a spectacular magical artifact. While you rested, I took time to examine it. The steel is like nothing I have ever seen. It has a perfect luster to it. I would say that it is indestructible. You said it could magnify the power of the one that wields it, but I could not make it work for me. How is it done?"

Japheth was hesitant. He did not fear Godun because he had been kind and gracious, but there was something about the situation that made him uneasy. "That's not exactly what I said. It can magnify the power of the one that *it* chooses to wield it."

Godun looked at him curiously and asked, "*It* chooses?"

"Yes," Japheth replied. "There is only one at a time, it is passed down from family member to family member as it chooses."

Godun thought for a few moments and asked, "Has anyone outside of your family ever used it to increase their power?"

"No, not once since Merlin forged it. Others have handled the sword, but it has never enhanced anyone's power except for the one it chooses."

Godun squinted his eyes as if searching for a thought, stroking his beard he said, "Interesting. How do you know this?"

"It's recorded in our family book," he answered. "It is a complete history of my family from the time of Merlin until now."

Godun walked to Japheth and handed him Lux. Japheth grasped and sheathed it. Having Lux back in his possession made him feel much more comfortable. With the temporary worry ended Japheth's thoughts moved quickly back to the book.

"Can I look at the book again?" Japheth asked.

"Most certainly," Godun replied. He motioned for Japheth to return to the table.

Japheth moved to the table where the book sat open just as he had left it. It occurred to him that being in the cave, he had no sense of how long he had slept, or what time of the day it was. It was a slight concern that quickly melted away as he began reading in the book once more.

Japheth began reading through the spells portion of the book. As he did, he saw many spells that he recognized and many more that he did not. Each one had the word, or words to be spoken, along with notation on how to properly pronounce it. If the spell was only slightly mispronounced it would not work, so having this knowledge was vital to Japheth. Some spells seemed fairly innocent, like one to make one's self invisible. To ones that seemed almost unthinkable, like the spell that would open a rift in the earth.

Japheth looked up from the book to ask Godun if there was some way he could write a few of the spells down to take home so that he wouldn't be forced to memorize them. He knew that if he couldn't review them, he would most likely get the pronunciation wrong. He looked around the cave, but Godun was nowhere to be seen.

He didn't want to leave the book, but he compelled himself to rise and search for Godun. He exited the cave expecting it to be midday, but he noticed that it was almost sunset. He looked around but could still not see Godun.

He walked out to where the mountain slope began and looked

down the hill. He saw Godun sitting next to his dragon. Grunge was still mostly buried by the loose fragments of the mountain, but his head was uncovered, and it appeared that Godun was petting him as he spoke.

Japheth started down the hill and both Grunge and Godun turned to look. When he reached them he spoke, "Godun I was wondering if you had any paper that I could write some information from the book down on. I don't think that I can remember the spells well enough to not foul them up when I get home."

Godun nodded his head and said, "Yes I believe I have some small fragments of paper that you could use."

Japheth noticed that Grunge was looking at him. It was not a hostile look, but more inquisitive. "Is he your pet?"

Godun replied, "No, pet would not be the right word. A companion would be more accurate. We have been together for a long time, and we understand and respect each other. Grunge would give his life for me, and I for him. I saved him from Ferox when he was just a whelp. Because he could not fly, he was abandoned by his mother. I knew the value he possessed and so I brought him here.

"I don't know that he has saved my life, but there have been many times when he has given me some much-needed assistance. Would you like to pet him?"

The question caught Japheth off guard.

Godun followed up his question with an explanation. "It's quite alright. If I tell him you are a friend he will not harm you."

Japheth nodded his head and said, "Yes, I would."

Godun leaned over to Grunge and spoke to him. Japheth could hear him, but he did not understand the words he used, he knew it must have been a language that he did not know. When he finished he motioned for Japheth to move forward.

Japheth slowly moved towards Grunge and put his hand on the large dragon's forehead and stroked down to his nose. After he rubbed his head a few more times, Grunge made a low humming sound, almost like the purr of a cat, and seemed to smile at Japheth.

Japheth returned the smile.

"He likes you," Godun said.

"That's good, I hate to think what would happen to me if he didn't," Japheth replied.

Japheth stopped petting Grunge and the great dragon nudged him with the end of his snout, nearly knocking him over. Japheth stood and looked at Godun, dismissing the playful gesture from Grunge. "Can I get that paper now? I'd really like to continue on with my study of the book."

"Yes, let's go back to the cave. Are you hungry?"

Again, Japheth hadn't noticed that he had not eaten in some time and didn't realize he was hungry until after Godun had asked him.

"Yes, I am hungry, I have some of my own food, I don't need to inconvenience you."

Godun replied, "It's no inconvenience at all, you saw how easy it is for me to produce food for a meal."

The pair walked back into the cave, Japheth sat at the book, and Godun brought him a small slip of paper, and a writing quill with ink.

"Thank you," Japheth said kindly. He turned back to the book to begin copying down spells.

Godun stopped him before he had written anything. "You may want to read through it completely before you write anything down. That is the only piece of paper I have for you. You should make sure you get whatever is most important to you written down. If you begin writing now you may not have room for something that you really need."

Godun's words rang true and Japheth put the quill down and began reading once again. In what seemed like only a few moments Godun had a plate of fresh vegetables in front of him.

"You had better eat before you get too engrossed in your studies again," Godun suggested.

Japheth looked at the plate with contempt. He wanted nothing but to read the book, but the growling of his stomach at the sight of the food convinced him otherwise.

"Thank you," he said, and quickly ate the meal. He devoured the rest of the book with an insatiable appetite. As he did, he tried to make a mental note of the spells that he would most like to have. He knew there were far too many for him to write down on the limited amount of space that he had.

As he finished an odd notion came to his mind. Godun professed to be at least hundreds of years old, yet he had not seen anything in the book that would help him to achieve this.

Japheth looked up to see Godun seated, watching him.

The obvious look of confusion on his face gave his thoughts away to Godun.

"You look puzzled my young friend."

Japheth replied, "I am somewhat puzzled. You claim to be very old, and I believe you, but I don't see anything in this book that would help you become immortal."

Godun chuckled then said, "I am not immortal, but I have learned of a substance that will make one nearly immortal. I discovered it from a deep study of the book, but I have chosen not to put it in the book in simple terms, to keep its composition a secret."

"It's a potion then?" Japheth asked.

"Yes, it's a potion, with many extremely rare, and hard to procure ingredients. The most important of them all is shavings from a particular stone. It also is difficult to concoct correctly. If done incorrectly the results can be rather incendiary. I call it lapis philosophorum."

"Would you share the recipe with me?" Japheth asked.

Very bluntly, but kindly Godun answered, "No. If this substance was discovered by the kings of the world, I fear it would be devastating."

"But if this potion could be made and given to everyone, people would not know death," Japheth argued.

Godun returned, "True, but that is not the only thing the potion will do, let me show you."

Godun walked to the shelves and grabbed a porcelain bowl, and one of the potion bottles. He put a small ingot of lead into the bowl and poured a meager amount of the thick liquid on the lead. Then he covered the bowl with a cloth. After a few moments smoke began to emerge from under the cloth. Then without warning the cloth burst into flames, which were gone in an instant.

When Japheth leaned over to look into the bowl, he could feel the heat radiating from it. As he looked into the bowl, he expected to see the lead melted, instead, he saw what looked like gold. Surprised, Japheth looked up at Godun.

"You didn't just turn that lead into gold did you?"

"Yes, that is exactly what happened," Godun replied.

After the amazement left, Japheth realized how this potion could be the cause of untold wars and contentions among men. With it, one could become infinitely rich, and powerful men would stop at nothing to have it.

Godun interrupted Japheth in his thoughts. "There are many more things it can be used for, some are far less spectacular, of course." Godun motioned to the lamps burning in the cave. "These lamps have been burning since you came here. Have you seen me refill them?"

Japheth shook his head and said, "No."

"That's because they are filled with the potion. They only need be filled once for they will burn forever.

"There is not enough time in a day to discuss what the potion can or might be used for, so I suggest you get back to the book."

His mind had been briefly distracted from the book, and when Godun mentioned it Japheth's thoughts moved back to the spells that he would like to write down.

Japheth began searching through the book again for the spells he had mentally noted that he felt would be of most use. On the small piece of paper, he was only able to write down four spells, with their pronunciation, and how to properly cast them. Until now he had only known spells that you needed to speak, but some required movements for them to work correctly.

The first spell was festinent. He thought that it would allow him to speed up, as Lux had helped him to do multiple times.

The next was motus. It was a spell to make the earth shake and move as if water.

Occipitalis was the next spell he wrote down. It would cause the earth to open and spread apart.

The final spell he wrote down was invisibilia. It would allow him to become invisible.

One spell that he needn't write down was sana. This was a spell that Japheth's family had used in the past. It could be used to help heal minor cuts and wounds, as well as stop infection, but the spell would not work on injuries sustained from magic. They had tried the spell to heal his aunt Deborah's burns, as well as his father's wounds, but it hadn't worked either time. The book stated that if the one casting the spell, touched the wound with both hands, major injuries could be healed. When he read this, he thought of Thaddeus.

Satisfied that he had copied the spells that would help him the most he looked up from his work.

Godun was in the cave reading from a small book.

Once he had his spells written down, his thoughts moved back to the potion that Godun had shown him. If Godun would not share the recipe, maybe he would give Japheth a small amount of it.

Japheth spoke tentatively, "Godun?"

Godun looked up from his book.

He continued, "Would you consider giving me a small amount of the lapis philosophorum?"

Godun looked suspiciously at Japheth, "Why did you come here?"

"I was in search of the book," Japheth answered.

Godun's eyes narrowed. "Is that really why, or were you searching for lapis philosophorum?"

Japheth was taken back by Godun's reaction. "No, I didn't even know it existed until you showed it to me."

Godun rose to his feet. "If that is so we shall find out now."

Godun reached out his hand and Japheth found himself unable to move. Godun moved to the shelves and pulled a potion from them. He walked to Japheth, opened his mouth and placed a drop on his tongue. The potion was putrid. Had Japheth had control over his body he would have heaved.

He stood and watched Japheth for a few moments. Then he stooped down and looked Japheth in the eyes. "Now tell me, what brought you to this place?"

Japheth answered involuntarily, "I came in search of the book."

"Why did you seek the book?"

Again, Japheth was not able to control his speech. "To find an antidote for dragonsbane."

His answer surprised Godun. He stepped back and released his spell on Japheth.

He vomited.

"Why did you do that?" Japheth demanded, still hunched over.

"I'm sorry, I have become more jaded by the visitors from the past. Most of my visitors are wizards or alchemists trying to find a way to make lapis philosophorum. You seemed to be genuine in your desire, but when you wanted some of the potion, I doubted my initial assessment of you. I had to be sure that you weren't trying to deceive me.

"Once, many years ago, I gave some of the potion to a man that I thought would be my apprentice. He sneaked away with it, and my staff, in the night, and I fear that my decision to give him some may be to my detriment. That potion could be devastating in the wrong hands, and I worry this his are the wrong hands.

"Why would you need an antidote for dragonsbane?"

Godun's question snapped Japheth's mind back to why he had come. He had been so spellbound by Godun and the book that he had lost sight of why he had made the difficult journey. For an instant he pictured his aunt Deborah, suffering from the effects of the drangonsbane, and guilt filled his conscience.

He looked up at Godun. "My aunt has burns from preparing it. She cannot find any relief, and I was hoping to find something in the book to help her."

Godun looked at Japheth for a few moments. "The only thing

that will help here is the lapis philosophorum. Healing is one of its properties."

He moved to the shelves and pulled off the potion and another small corked vial. Japheth watched as he allowed one drop to pass from the large bottle to the small one, then he replaced the cork.

Handing it to Japheth he said, "Fill a bucket with water and thoroughly mix this in with it. Have your aunt wipe down her body with the water and she will be cured."

Japheth's heart leapt in his chest. "Thank you, oh thank you," he said as he placed the vial in his pocket.

"Why was your aunt preparing dragonsbane?" Godun asked. "That isn't a substance that one wants to experiment with."

"We needed it to combat some dragons," Japheth answered.

Godun looked puzzled and asked, "Where would you come across dragons?"

"They came to us. Our town was attacked."

"Why didn't you defeat them with your sword?" Godun inquired.

"I didn't have it at the time. It was stolen by the man that attacked our town, Vesuvius," Japheth answered.

Godun stood frozen, not believing what he had heard. "Did you say that Vesuvius attacked your town?"

"Yes, why?"

Godun continued, "That is the man I thought would be my apprentice, the one with the lapis philosophorum. What happened to the dragons and Vesuvius?"

Japheth told Godun the story from beginning to end. He started with the change in the forest animals and continued to when he defeated Vesuvius.

Godun listened intently, never interrupting Japheth. After he had finished Godun asked, "So you saw Vesuvius' body then?"

"Well, I didn't see it. I lost consciousness for three days, but everyone said all that was left was his burnt cloak."

Godun stroked his beard and somberly spoke, "Japheth, I don't believe Vesuvius is dead."

CHAPTER 24

Vesuvius lay face down, motionless on the cold stone floor. Crag moved swiftly down the damp steps to where he lay. Crag secured his torch on the wall and bent down to examine his master. He rolled Vesuvius over. His body was cool to the touch. His breaths were short and shallow, but he was still breathing.

Crag carefully picked him up and carried him up the long dim staircase to a lavishly furnished room. He set him gingerly on a large bed, pulled some blankets up onto him, and lit a fire to warm his chambers.

Crag spent the next few hours preparing food and bringing water to the room so that he would be ready to help Vesuvius if he should wake. He dressed the wound on Vesuvius' hand where Japheth's knife had pierced it. For the remainder of the day, Crag sat patiently by his bedside, but he did not stir. Crag slept on the floor next to the fire until he woke the next day, still, there was no movement from Vesuvius.

Another fire was built, and Crag resumed waiting, to no avail. The day came and went with no improvement. Crag was starting to lose hope that Vesuvius would recover.

Sometime in the night, Crag was awakened by a low, weak moan from Vesuvius. Crag rose and moved to his master's side. Though the room was almost completely black, Crag could see that Vesuvius was moving. He lit the lamp on the table. As the dim light invaded the darkness, Vesuvius opened his eyes.

"Master, you're alive," Crag said quietly.

"That boy," Vesuvius frailly muttered, "is going to pay. Him and that whole miserable village."

"How can that be?" Japheth exclaimed.

"There is a very powerful potion and spell combination that I taught Vesuvius. You would use the potion to enchant an area. If needed, you then use a spell that will transport only your body to the enchanted area.

"The process can be nearly lethal, and the time it would take to recover could be extensive, but if you did not see his body, I would guess that he used this tactic to escape you."

Only a few moments earlier Japheth had been elated to learn that he could help his aunt Deborah, now he felt the darkest feelings of panic and despair rush over him.

Japheth spoke with alarm, "I have to get back to warn Licentia, and to face Vesuvius if he comes again."

Godun placed his hand on Japheth's shoulder and spoke. "I understand your eagerness to return home but let me speak to you for a few moments. I have been on this earth for hundreds of years. I have seen kingdoms rise and fall. The one thing that is consistent with men is that there will always be someone trying to control the masses. Most do it physically, some try to mentally. If Vesuvius is successful, he will be the ruler. If he is not, similar threats will come from elsewhere, if they are defeated a new tyrant will arise, and the cycle goes on and on. The only reprieve that comes to man is when a benevolent leader somehow gains control. Those in control resort to all kinds of intrigue to gain power and rarely can a good man grasp, let alone retain, control.

"I can offer you something different, something better. Here on Black Mountain, we are free from the fruitless struggles of men. If you stay with me, I can teach you the secrets I have learned through lifetimes of study. I will share the lapis philosophorum, and eventually, I will teach you how to make it.

"While it is true that I am not immortal I believe that with enough study, I, or we I should say, can become such.

"I know it is a hard thing that I ask of you. Leaving your family behind is difficult, I know from my own sad sacrifices, but if you leave, I do not think you will ever come back because you cannot defeat Vesuvius. He is a much stronger wizard than you, even with the help of your sword.

"He has my staff, which, like your sword, magnifies your powers and abilities. I could defeat him with great difficulty if the need arises, but I do not see that day ever coming.

"Of course, you are free to leave, but I would ask that you stay and become my apprentice. What do you say young Japheth?"

Japheth was only slightly surprised by Godun's offer. A similar idea had crossed his mind as he spent time studying. He was infatuated by the book, and it pained him to think about leaving it, but he knew he could not abandon his family. The choice was easy for Japheth to make because he had already made it.

"I appreciate your offer Godun, but I have a responsibility to my family to return to them. My aunt Deborah needs this cure. The people of my town will depend on me to defeat Vesuvius, and if we are not successful, I will feel peace in the fact that we stood together for our freedom."

Godun nodded his head knowingly. He had been faced with a similar decision many years ago.

"I see you are determined in your decision, and I can understand your reasons. If you must go, I will help you have somewhat of a chance against Vesuvius. If you were to be on the brink of defeating him, as you were before, he could simply transport himself again to escape you.

"To defeat him you would either need to know where he transports himself to, or you will need to prevent it.

"As you know every spell has a counter of some type. The spell Vesuvius uses is countered not by another spell, but by a potion."

Godun crossed the room to the shelves and handed Japheth a small bottle filled with a dark red liquid. "If the smallest amount of this potion comes into contact with his skin, he will be unable to transport himself away."

Japheth it took it gratefully. "Thank you Godun. I don't know how I'll use this successfully, but I have a few days of walking and riding to figure it out."

Japheth rose, put on his cloak, carefully put the piece of paper with the new spells on them in a concealed pocket, and prepared to leave. As he walked towards the entrance to the cave Godun sidestepped into his path.

"My young friend I admire your desire to help, and fight for your family, but I simply cannot let you leave with your sword. As you have probably noticed many of the artifacts mentioned in the book are in this cave. As I find clues to their location I go and get them. I also have procured many books like your family has. Sometimes the task is easy and sometimes it requires," Godun paused uncomfortably, "unsavory actions."

Japheth replied, "Do you mean you steal them, or do you forcibly take them?"

"I do whatever it takes, but most of the time they can be bought.

"If they cannot be bought, I will do what I need to, to get them. I believe in being peaceful, for the most part, but after all I have sacrificed for the knowledge in the book, I can justify almost anything to get what I feel I deserve.

"Your sword is a more magnificent relic than I have ever learned of in all of my studies. If I allow it out of here, I shall forever regret it. Therefore, you are free to leave, but the sword stays with me. I will, of course, compensate you for it." Godun dropped a large coin pouch on the table. It appeared to be completely full.

"I have not had the time to make this gold into coins. However, I doubt you will have a hard time getting people to take it. There is enough here for you to be considered a very wealthy man."

In an instant, Japheth's mind raced through possible ways to escape. He knew he could not hope to defeat Godun, either physically or magically. Trickery would be his only chance. Japheth recalled the pouch of dragonsbane tied to his belt, next to his sheath. He decided this would be his best opportunity.

He bowed his head slightly and moved his hands as if to pull Lux from his sheath. In one fluid motion, he grasped the pouch, ripped it from his belt, and flung the opened end across his body towards Godun.

Only a small amount of the powder escaped the pouch, but it was enough. Godun's demeanor changed from one of confidence, to one of rage. He grabbed Japheth's arm with alarming quickness. His grip was so powerful that it seemed as if it would crush Japheth's arm. His lips curled in anger and he exclaimed, "That was your last mistake my friend!" That is when the burning began.

Godun continued to hold Japheth's arm, but his grip loosened a little. He brought his off hand up to his face and tried to wipe it off. When that didn't work, he started pulling Japheth towards the shelves. He started making some painful grunting noises. The drangonsbane had gotten into his eyes.

Japheth jerked his arm out of Godun's grasp and ran to the entrance of the cave. He paused and turned back towards him. "It's drangonsbane," he said before he left the cave and began running down the mountainside.

He could hear Godun screaming behind him, but he could not make out the words. The ruckus had aroused Grunge, who removed himself from the mountainside. As Japheth approached, Grunge looked at him quizzically. Japheth stopped and pointed towards the cave. "Help Godun."

The great dragon turned his huge head and looked towards the cave. As Godun's screaming reached them something in Grunge changed. He slowly looked back at Japheth with his lips in a snarl. The beast released a monstrous bellow and took in a massive breath to breath fire at Japheth.

Without hesitation, Japheth hit Grunge with the inpulsa spell. The shock caused Grunge to fall in a heap to the ground.

As Godun's anger raged inside the cave, dark, almost completely black, storm clouds began to gather around the peak of Black Mountain.

Japheth moved speedily down the hill. In a few moments, he could hear that Grunge had recovered and was pursuing him. He looked over his shoulder to see Grunge quickly closing the gap between them. He stopped and turned to face him.

Japheth cast the conglacior spell and immediately Grunge again fell to the earth. His extremities had begun freezing. Japheth continued casting the spell until Grunge had become completely incapacitated, but not killed.

Hoping that he would not need to confront Grunge again, he continued down the mountain.

The storm clouds that were gathering had almost completely blocked out the light of the sun. The clouds had also begun to release a torrid rainfall, almost hot to the touch, which made traveling down the hill more difficult. Steam rose from the ground as the rain hit.

Japheth heard Grunge roar angrily, and he knew that he would not allow Japheth to escape him.

Japheth turned to face the dragon once more. He used the conglacior spell again, only this time he cast it to completion.

Grunge slumped to the earth and slid down the mountain, coming to a stop in the loose fragments of earth only feet from Japheth. He could see the rage in the dragon's eyes, and he felt pity for the beast. He knew Grunge was just protecting his master.

As Japheth continued casting the spell, the brute became completely frozen over. In only a few more short moments Grunge's body exploded into fragments of ice, and scattered about the mountainside.

With some sadness in his heart, he continued working his way down. He remembered what Godun had told him about leaving Ferox, and so he made his way towards the desert.

Having a great sense of urgency, he feared that he would not reach Licentia in time to stop Vesuvius. He knew he must get there as fast as he could, so he tried the festinent spell. The same tingling sensation that he had felt before came over his body and he moved with an unnatural speed and quickness towards the desert.

The rain continued to fall in sheets, but the bizarre temperature of the rain had changed from exceedingly hot, to frigid. The rain penetrated his clothing and chilled his skin. In what seemed like only a few minutes he had reached the base of the mountain, and before him lay the utter wasteland of the desert.

Taking only a few moments to rest, he drew his sword in preparation for what may lie ahead. He knew he must continue in his accelerated state until he found Thaddeus. Not knowing exactly how long he had been with Godun, he hoped that Thaddeus was still waiting for him with the horses.

Japheth burst from his spot and moved as quickly as he could through the desert.

The soft sand made running more difficult, but because of his quickened pace, it was not as cumbersome as it would have been otherwise.

His clothing was saturated with the cold rain that continued to pour, and as he continued the added weight began to make him tire. The thoughts of his family and town being vulnerable to Vesuvius drove him on.

As he saw the beginnings of a tree line in the distance it lifted his spirits. Godun had been right about the desert being an easier route. Even though he had to run in the rain through most of the night he had not encountered any of the fearful creatures of Ferox.

Just as this thought entered his head the ground beneath his feet shifted. He lost his footing and rolled to the ground. From the corner of his eye, he saw a snake, as big around as a man, rise up from under the wet sand.

The huge serpent struck quickly at Japheth. He rolled and wildly swung his arm behind him. As luck would have it, the snake's head hit where his body had been, and his sword cleanly removed its head.

Japheth was up in a flash only to find that he had dispatched the deadly viper almost by accident.

Breathing an exhausted sigh of relief, he continued working his way out of the desert and back to Thaddeus.

He left the desert and then headed east towards where he thought Thaddeus would be waiting for him. He saw what he thought was a slender column of smoke, rising above the trees in the distance. He was exhausted, but he pushed himself on, knowing that he may only have enough stamina to make it to the smoke he had seen.

As he entered the small clearing, he was overjoyed to see Thaddeus kneeling by the fire. He stopped, and the effect of the festinent spell ended. He dropped to the ground, exhausted and nearly unconscious.

Thaddeus rushed to his side, and with the last bit of strength he had he looked up and said, "We have to get back to Licentia, Vesuvius is not dead." After Japheth had spoken those words his world went black.

CHAPTER 25

Japheth woke with a start. He tried to rise but found that he could not. As his eyes adjusted, he could see that he was on a horse. He lifted his head and could see Thaddeus riding in front leading his horse.

"Thaddeus," he said weakly, "help me."

Thaddeus looked over his shoulder and smiled. He brought the horses to a stop and dismounted. He walked back and untied Japheth.

Japheth slid from the saddle and hit the ground. His wobbly legs could not bear his weight and he fell to the earth.

Thaddeus chuckled and extended a hand to Japheth. Japheth reached for it and found himself jerked to his feet. He managed to stay upright this time.

"I'm glad to see you awake, I was beginning to wonder if you would sleep the entire trip home."

"How long have I been asleep?" Japheth asked.

"Two days. When you came into camp you said something about Vesuvius, and then passed out." A more serious look came across Thaddeus' face. "I figured since James was not with you, he would not be making the trip back with us."

Japheth's eyes fell to the ground and he nodded. "You're right Thaddeus, he died in the swamp, saving me."

Thaddeus spoke softly, "Then he made good on his oath to your father." He continued, "I wasn't' sure what to make of you babbling on about Vesuvius, but I figured since you didn't have the book, we must be going home. You seemed very intent in your desire to get back to Licentia, so instead of waiting for you to rest I tied you to your horse and started back."

Japheth's mind recovered from its daze and he looked intensely at Thaddeus. He shook his head as if to clear the mist from it. "Thaddeus, Vesuvius may not be dead."

"How can that be?" he asked. "No one could survive that lightning strike."

"I did," Japheth returned.

"Touche," Thaddeus returned, still not believing Japheth.

Japheth continued, "Thaddeus, I found the book, but it was not abandoned in a cave. The man that took it there, Godun, still guards it today. Vesuvius was a pupil of his, and he told me about a spell that Vesuvius could have used to escape the lightning. We have to get back to Licentia quickly."

Thaddeus' voice took on a more serious tone. "Are you sure Japheth? How can that possibly be?"

"I am sure, and I will tell you more about it as we ride, but we can't afford to delay, we must ride now."

Japheth looked at Thaddeus' broken arm. "Before we get off, let me see if I can heal that."

"Why didn't you do that before?" Thaddeus asked.

"I didn't know how. We have a spell that can be used to treat small wounds, but nothing major. The book taught me how to heal more severe injuries."

Japheth took Thaddeus' broken arm in his hands and cast the sana spell.

Thaddeus' head perked up. "My arm is getting warm," he said. Then there appeared to be a slight glow that looked like it was coming from under his skin for a few brief moments. Japheth withdrew his hand.

Thaddeus opened and closed his fist a few times. Then he rotated his arm while he bent and straightened it again and again. He looked at Japheth in amazement. "There's no more pain," he said.

"Good, then lets start for home," Japheth said.

As the men rode towards Licentia, Japheth rehearsed the entire story to Thaddeus. He included every detail that he could remember. Then he pulled the paper from his pocket with the new spells written on it.

"I think these spells could be especially useful if I have to fight Vesuvius again, they are all I could write down from the book."

Thaddeus suggested that Japheth practice them on the ride. "From my limited magical experience, I know that you cannot just pick those up and be proficient with them. Use these next couple of days to really know those spells."

Japheth took Thaddeus' advice. He knew that the festinent spell worked. He could not practice casting the motus, or occipitalis spells while riding his horse, but he did practice the invisibilia spell. At first, he could only make his body invisible, but after a few hours his clothes, and then the horse would become invisible as well.

When they stopped to make camp for the night, Japheth wanted to try the other two spells. He spoke the motus spell and nothing happened. He drew Lux and spoke it again. He felt a slight tremor beneath his feet. Remembering that some spells needed actions to work, he drove Lux into the ground and uttered it a third time. The ground began to buck and jump in a way that neither Japheth nor Thaddeus had ever experienced. As soon as Japheth removed his sword from the earth, the motion ceased.

Thaddeus sat wide eyed, staring at Japheth.

"What was that?" he said in a way that wasn't really a question. The amazement was evident in his voice. "Did that man on the mountain teach you that?"

"No, he didn't help me with it at all."

Thaddeus asked, "What else do you have to practice?"

"I have one more that will supposedly open a crack in the earth."

Thaddeus moved to Japheth's side and instructed him to direct his focus away from where the horses were tied.

Japheth held Lux in his hand and spoke the occipitalis spell, nothing happened. He again drove Lux into the ground as he spoke, and a fissure began where Lux penetrated the earth and moved outward. At its widest point, it was over ten feet wide, and the bottom could not be seen.

Both Thaddeus and Japheth were shocked, and maybe even a little alarmed at the result.

Thaddeus spoke first, "It's too bad you couldn't have brought that book back with you."

"Yes, it is. I was just lucky to get away from Godun at all."

The night came and went without incident, and their travel towards Licentia the following day went smoothly as well.

As they rode, Japheth wondered if he could get the invisibilia spell to work only on something else, or if he also had to be made invisible. Japheth struggled for most of the day trying to make his horse disappear, without disappearing himself. He had not made it work all day.

When they were about to stop and make camp for the night Japheth tried once more. He closed his eyes and ever so faintly muttered the spell while concentrating on his horse. When he opened his eyes, he appeared to be floating. He called to Thaddeus for verification.

"Thaddeus, can you see my horse?"

Thaddeus turned back to look. "I cannot," he said with astonishment. "It looks like you have gotten that spell to work as you'd hoped.

"If you are done playing around, I guess we should stop for the night."

As they made camp Japheth became restless, he knew that they would reach Licentia the following day. He felt some anxiety that they may not arrive before Vesuvius. He wanted to forego sleep and continue on. "Thaddeus, do you think we could ride through the night in order to get to Licentia sooner?"

Thaddeus replied, "I do not think it would be best. Our horses are tired and need to rest. If we did get there early tomorrow, we would be worn out as well, and if what you have told me about Vesuvius is true you would stand little chance against him."

"I stand little chance against him as it is," Japheth returned.

"I think you underestimate yourself. You nearly defeated him once, not by superior physical or magical skills, but by surprising him, by out thinking him. He may be the superior wizard, but I believe you are the superior person.

"Take the time you have left to design a way to defeat him. We still have to find a way to get the potion on him so he can't escape you again."

As Japheth sat around the fire that night, he tried to think of a way that he could defeat Vesuvius. He knew that getting the potion on him would be necessary in order to be successful. He and Thaddeus talked back and forth about different tactics that might be used. They struggled to come up with something that they were confident would work. Finally, Thaddeus had an idea. "If all else fails, give me the potion and I will get close enough to get it in contact with him."

"But how will you do that?" Japheth asked.

"I don't know. I do know that my desire to see Vesuvius defeated exceeds yours, and there is little that I cannot do when properly motivated."

The night proved uneventful, and the two men rose before they normally would in order to get an early start for Licentia. As they road, Japheth had an idea.

He was able to wound Vesuvius with a throwing knife disguised as a ball of fire. He wondered if Aaron could make an arrow out of metal. One that was extremely thin that he could still shoot a short distance with his bow. If he dipped the arrow in the potion and was able to hit Vesuvius he could get it to contact him. He ran the idea by Thaddeus as they traveled.

"I believe you may have something there. I'm not sure it would work, but if Aaron can make one light enough that you could still fire accurately, I think it would have a fine chance of working."

The closer they got to Licentia the antsier Japheth got. When the town came into sight, they quickened their pace. They were stopped only momentarily by the watchmen, then allowed to continue.

As the sun was getting low in the sky, they reached town, dismounted their horses, and Eli, still hobbling, was there to greet them. He walked to Japheth and embraced him in a strong, fatherly hug.

"Japheth, I'm so glad to see you're alright," he said.

Japheth smiled at his father. There was a bit of concern in his voice. "I am happy to be home. You haven't recovered yet?" he asked.

"No," Eli replied, "and I fear they I may not ever totally recover." He did not allow this fact to dampen his spirits. His son was home and he felt a great relief wash over him.

"Where is mother, and aunt Deborah?" Japheth inquired. "I have a cure for the drangonsbane." He pulled out the bottle that contained the drop of lapis philosophorum and showed it to his father.

Eli responded, "They are at the house. It is good that you have returned. The effect of the dragonsbane is getting worse. Your aunt Deborah is in a great deal of pain."

"Please take me to her," Japheth requested.

Father and son quickly made their way to the house. As they did Japheth gave Eli a summarized version of what had happened in Ferox. As they reached the house Japheth said, "I can tell you the details in a few moments." Japheth pushed open the door. "Hello mother," he said.

Abigail surged to her feet and embraced her son. "I am so happy to see you son."

"I am happy to be home," he said with a smile, releasing his mother. "I have the antidote for aunt Deborah."

"Then you found the book?" she asked with excitement. "Where is it?"

"Yes, I found it, but I do not have it with me. The experience was not as remarkable as you might think. Quickly, let's get aunt Deborah the cure for the drangonsbane."

Debora was lying in bed in a room in the back. The relief that they had for the burning was becoming less and less effective, and she was perpetually in pain. Japheth noticed that she looked exhausted. He guessed it must be because she was not sleeping much.

He hurriedly mixed the lapis philosophorum as Godun had instructed him. Abigail then used a rag to wipe down Deborah's hands and arms where the dragonsbane had contacted her skin. She was brought immediate relief. In just a few minutes she was sleeping soundly.

Abigail embraced her son once more. "Thank you, oh thank you Japheth. Thank you for coming home and thank you for helping Deborah. I think if you had not found this cure, the dragonsbane would have eventually taken her life, only after a great deal of suffering."

Japheth could sense the relief in his mother's voice.

"Well son, sit and tell me all about your grand adventure," she said happily.

Japheth looked at his mother in a way that communicated things did not go as well as she assumed.

The family gathered around in their house and Japheth went over what had happened in Ferox. He took his time and hit every detail from the time they left until he and Thaddeus had reentered town. He told of the gruesome beats that he had seen in Ferox, and how James had sacrificed himself for Japheth. He told of the wonders that Godun kept within the cave, and how the possibilities of what could be done seemed endless. He also included what Godun had offered him, how he had tried to take Lux, and his escape from Ferox. The tale took hours to tell. When he finished the family sat in stunned silence.

Eli was the first to speak. "Well you know what this means, we have to prepare to face Vesuvius again." His voice sounded discouraged, but not beaten.

"Father," Japheth said, "I think I know how, but I have to go see Aaron."

Eli nodded knowingly, "Alright son, but it best wait 'til morning."

CHAPTER 26

J apheth slept well. He was exhausted from his journey, and the night came and went in an instant. No startling dreams or premonitions bothered his sleep for the first night since Vesuvius' army had come to their town. He woke up feeling peaceful and refreshed.

He left his bedroom to find his family eating breakfast.

Abigail was the first to greet him, "It looks like you had a fine sleep."

"Yes mother I did," Japheth replied as he rubbed the sleep from his eyes. He looked at Eli, "Can we go see Aaron now?"

Eli smiled at his son. "Give the man a chance to wake up and get moving for the day. Sit and eat, and then we'll go."

Japheth sat down and quickly ate his food, when he finished Eli was waiting. They started through town towards the blacksmith's shop and reached it in a few minutes. Aaron was already there working.

Japheth explained his experience of the last couple weeks to Aaron. He concluded with the idea that if Aaron could make an arrow small and light enough that Japheth could put the potion on it and hit Vesuvius with it, stopping him from escaping as he had before.

Aaron thought for a few moments, then spoke. "I think I can make you what you need, however it will take some time. Getting the arrow thin, and light enough to shoot shouldn't be much of a problem but keeping it straight so that you can hit something with it may be more difficult.

"Also, I think the town needs to know what is going on. There has been some speculation surrounding your return. It would be best to gather everyone in and tell them what you have told me. We need to prepare to face Vesuvius again."

Eli agreed with Aaron. "Aaron you get to work on the arrow, maybe try to make two, and we'll gather everyone together and let them know what to expect with Vesuvius."

Japheth and Eli went home and enlisted the entire family to get the word out for everyone to meet at noon. They soon spread throughout the town, and at noon the entire town was gathered at the square.

Eli's booming voice quieted the rumbling sea of voices of the crowd. "Licentians, we have begun rebuilding our town with the thought that we were free from the dangers we faced. My son Japheth left in pursuit of a book of knowledge. During his search, he has learned that Vesuvius may not be dead, and if he is not, we must prepare to face him yet again."

The crowd, which had been silent, began to reverberate with anonymous voices. Most speaking to their neighbor, or no one in particular.

Eli's commanding voice again quieted the crowd. "I will let Japheth fill you in on what he has learned."

Japheth stood and began telling his story again. He did not yet have the powerful voice of his father, but he continued as loudly as he could. He left out many of the details that he had used in retelling his story previously. He felt that time was short, and most of the details were not pertinent to preparing for Vesuvius.

When he finished there was only stunned silence. Eli reached out and grasped Japheth's shoulder. "Son, I will take over from here. Go see how Aaron is coming with those arrows."

Japheth gratefully nodded and began making his way to the blacksmith. As he left, he could hear many people from town, his father included, beginning to present ideas of what would be most critical to do.

Japheth knew that whatever the town could do would mean little in defeating Vesuvius. If they were going to be rid of him it would have to be him to do it. He began to feel the heavy weight of his responsibilities. His mind began racing again for ways that he could gain an advantage.

He became so lost in his thoughts that he nearly walked past the blacksmith shop. His head jerked up and he veered into the shop. It looked like Aaron was working on an arrow.

"How is it coming?" Japheth asked.

Aaron looked up from his work. "Fairly well I think." He held up a thin shaft with a pair of tongs. "I am having a little trouble keeping it straight, but I think I have it about as small as I can make it. I also need to add the fletching.

"If you and your father would come by in a couple hours, I will have one completed. I would like you to shoot it and get a feel for the range you will have with it. Then I can repair any damage to it, and it will be ready to use."

Japheth agreed and left for home. He wanted to ponder, he wanted to be alone so he could think. He walked to the house, but instead of going in he went around to the back. He slumped to the ground, brought his knees up to his chest, and began searching the horizon as if the answers to all his troubles could be found there.

How long he stared blankly he could not tell. His thoughts were as empty as his gaze. No answers were coming. No ideas were forming. The longer he sat, the more frustrated he became. His frustration was beginning to transform into discouragement. It started to seem to him as if there were no answers, no solutions.

His mother noticed him sitting, and she went outside to talk with him. When she rounded the corner, she could almost feel the pessimism radiating from him.

"What is the matter?" she asked kindly.

Japheth answered, "Nothing is really wrong. I'm just trying to think of a way to fool Vesuvius again. I don't know how I can defeat him."

"You don't have to do it alone, you have your family and everyone in the town, for that matter, to help you."

Japheth let his frustration seep into his words. "Mother I know that everyone is willing to help, but I don't think it will do any good. If he is going to be beat, it is me that has to do it."

Abigail replied gently, "Son you place too much responsibility on yourself. There is only so much you can do. No matter how powerful you think you are, you can accomplish more when you work with others."

"I know you're right mother, but I just can't see how anyone else can help. After reading the book and getting a glimpse of what is possible, I don't think that I can possibly stand up to him. I feel like anyone else would just be forfeiting their life if they try to face him."

"Perhaps you are right, but only if we were to face him individually, together we can be more. Don't be so quick to underestimate the abilities of those around you."

With those words, she left Japheth to his thoughts and returned to the house.

He sat a few moments, thinking about his mother's wise counsel. He got off the ground to go talk to her. As he came around the corner of the house, he saw his father walking towards him. Seeing him made his thoughts jump back to the arrow that Aaron was making.

He rushed to his father. "We need to go see Aaron with our bows. He will have an arrow finished by now. He said we should go by and fire it, to get a feel for how far we can shoot it accurately. Then if it is damaged, he can fix it before it is needed."

"Let's get our bows and go see if a blacksmith can make a better arrow than an archer," Eli said, only half kidding.

They retrieved their bows and arrived at the blacksmith shop in short order. There on the table sat a beautiful, nearly perfectly metal arrow. The extremely slender shaft looked too frail to hold up to being shot. If Japheth did not know better, he would have said that the fletching was made of feathers, not metal.

Aaron looked up and smiled. "You've come to try the arrow, let's go out back." Aaron picked up the arrow and they walked behind his shop to where he had a target set up. He turned and handed the arrow to Japheth.

Japheth took it and handed it to his father. Eli looked it over. "You certainly have made a fine arrow," he said as he looked down the shaft, inspecting how straight it was.

Aaron noticed his examination and said, "You'll find that it is not perfectly straight, but because you are not shooting it a great distance it should not make much of a difference."

Eli looked up and said jokingly, "I'll be the judge of that."

He knocked the arrow, took careful aim at the target roughly thirty yards away, and shot it. The arrow hit the target half a foot below the bullseye.

"Are you sure it wasn't your aim?" Aaron teased.

Without a word, Eli took an arrow from his quiver, and in one smooth, fluid motion nocked the arrow, and drew back his bow. He took his eyes from the target and looked at Aaron before he released. The arrow hit nearly dead center of the bullseye.

"I guess not," Aaron said in rebuttal to himself.

Japheth retrieved the arrow and Eli shot again. This time it hit just below his arrow in the bullseye.

"I think I have a fairly good idea of how that arrow will shoot. Japheth it's your turn."

Japheth was not able to compensate so quickly for the added weight of the special arrow. His first shot was about eight inches low. He reasoned it was because his bow was not as powerful as his fathers. With each shot, he got closer and closer to his mark. On his seventh shot, he was inside the bullseye.

Eli spoke counsel to his son, "Remember if you are firing arrows rapidly it will be difficult to adjust your aim when you fire this arrow. You may need to take an extra moment. It is better that you fire slightly slower but hit your mark than it is to fire quickly and miss.

"I want you to practice firing some of your regular arrows and then this one.

"Aaron, would it be alright for Japheth to stay here and practice a little before you repair the arrow?"

"Absolutely, Japheth just bring it in when you are finished."

Eli spoke again, "Aaron, would you be able to make another of these?"

Aaron grinned as he responded, "I have already started on another. It will be ready by tomorrow."

Japheth began practicing as his father had instructed. He was surprised at how difficult it was to adjust his aim for the heavier arrow. When he shot it alone, he could hit the bullseye nearly every time, but when he shot it immediately after his regular arrows, he seemed to either over, or under compensate for the added weight.

As the sun was getting low in the sky, he had finally been able to adjust his aim rapidly, although he was not as confident as he wanted to be.

He took the arrow into Aaron, who was still laboring in his shop.

"I'm sorry it has taken so long," he said to the large blacksmith.

"Not to worry Japheth, I have plenty to work on," Aaron replied as he took the arrow from Japheth's hand. He looked down the shaft to see that it had bent from the practice.

"Japheth, part of the reason could be that the shaft is curved. I will have it repaired in no time."

Aaron looked up from the arrow. "I think you should know that some in the town have been speculating that the reason Vesuvius attacked us and will come against us again, is because of you and your family.

"I believe it is nonsense, but people tend to look for someone to blame for their hardships. They want to attribute the difficulties of life to someone else. I don't think it will be a problem for you or your family, but I thought you should know.

"If it wasn't for your family, I don't think any of us would be here."

"Thank you, Aaron, I will be sure to tell my family."

"Stop back by in the morning to collect your arrows young man."

"Yes sir," Japheth replied.

Japheth walked back to his house surprised at Aaron's words. How could this town feel like it was his family's fault? As he walked, he began to feel anger towards the townspeople. When he had reached his house, he immediately told his family what Aaron had said. To his surprise, his family did not share his outrage.

Abigail said, "We were waiting for this to happen."

"What?" Japheth blurted out.

"Son, this is what has happened to my family for generations. People like to accuse those that are different for their troubles. Not all people mind you, but enough to make things very uncomfortable for those they identify as different.

"You shouldn't be too bothered by it, but more importantly don't let those accusations make you feel ill towards them. You of all of us can't afford to have that happen. If you want to draw on Lux's power, you can't have that in your mind."

The family spent the rest of the evening eating their meal and enjoying each other's company, not knowing that on the morrow Vesuvius would be upon them.

CHAPTER 27

Crag and Vesuvius rode their broad steeds towards Licentia. It was just those two, no men, no dragons, just a wizard and his trusted companion.

It had taken Vesuvius many days to recover from the power of the spell that delivered him from Japheth's lightning. Vesuvius didn't mind, it gave him time to think, to think of various ways to defeat the boy and his town.

At first, he had considered rounding up all the dragons he could, flying over, and burning the entire region to the ground. It would be easy. It would be complete, and there would be no escape. He would achieve his goal, but it was too simple. The boy would never know what was coming. But what was most objectionable is that if the boy died this way, he would never know that he hadn't stopped Vesuvius. They would never know that regardless of all their efforts he would continue on and bring all of humanity under his control. He believed it, and he wanted the Licentians, and that boy in particular, to know that he would ultimately conquer. They had to know it so that he would feel complete in his conquest.

His plans had been set back years. To gather more soldiers, he would have to wait for boys to grow to men, and that took time, too much time. No, for this gross inconvenience the demise of Licentia and their adolescent hero had to be satisfying. It had to be personal.

He planned to openly challenge the boy. He hoped to draw him away from his town and his people. He wanted to share how he had escaped and describe in detail what he would do to the town after he had killed him. He wanted that feeling of dread and helplessness to be the last thing the boy felt.

He also wanted that sword. In the short time he had it in his possession he had not been able to use it as the boy had. He could sense that there was great power within it, just waiting to be released. He was certain that if he could only obtain it again that he could unlock its power.

Vesuvius and Crag had ridden the majority of the way to Licentia in silence. Vesuvius was brooding over how to triumph over the town and didn't spend much time talking. Crag by his very nature did not talk much, and so there was little said between the two.

As night approached, they stopped to make camp.

"Tell me Crag, how long will it take to reach Licentia from here?"

"Master, I think if we arise early and continue at a steady pace we should be there by midday tomorrow."

Vesuvius smiled a wicked smile and said, "That will be perfect. It will give them one more glorious sunrise to behold before they are swept off their ground.

"Crag, I have been thinking. Tomorrow when I call the boy out of town and challenge him to a fight, I want you there. After I have explained to him everything that I intend to do I will nod towards him. At that point, you charge. He will undoubtedly try some magic, which won't work against you. He won't realize that until it is too late. I want you to disarm him, bring me his sword, and put him on his knees before me. I will... persuade him to tell me the secret of how to use the sword, and then I will destroy him at my pleasure."

"I will," was Crag's short reply.

Crag thought for a few moments and asked, "But what if he will not accept your challenge?"

"I believe he will. If not, we will work our way towards the town. Once I am close enough for my magic to reach Licentia, he will be compelled to accept."

Crag nodded his head in agreeance.

Vesuvius looked out in the direction of Licentia and with a devilish grin said, "I think I will allow a few people to escape so that they may spread the word of what I did to this town and those that opposed me. Tomorrow I claim my revenge, and Licentia will be no more."

CHAPTER 28

Japheth woke after a second peaceful night. He felt well rested and better than he had in a long while. He hurriedly made his way to Aaron's blacksmith shop. The respected smith was just starting a fire to begin working. He greeted Japheth cheerfully.

"Hello, young man. I assume you're here for the arrows."

"I am," Japheth replied.

"Well, I was able to finish them last night. They have had plenty of time to cool. They are ready for whatever you will face."

"Thank you Aaron, and thank you for warning me about what is being said about my family, and for trusting us."

Aaron responded, "I think people should be judged on their actions. Often people will say what others want to hear, but then their actions do not match their words. Your family's speech and actions are consistent, and that makes you easy to trust.

"Good luck with whatever you must encounter, I hope those arrows meet your expectations."

Japheth thanked Aaron again and left for home.

He walked through the door to find his entire family sitting at the table, and breakfast nearly prepared.

"I picked up the arrows from Aaron, I'd like to get the potion on them so it can be drying," he explained to his family.

Eli responded first, "I think that's a good idea. I'll come help."

Father and son went to the back room where the potion was kept.

Japheth removed the cork from the bottle and dipped the tip of the arrow in the potion.

Eli interrupted his actions. "I think we should coat the whole length of the arrows. You can't be sure if that will make a difference or not."

Japheth agreed, and they proceeded to put a coat over both arrows. They were left on the table to dry, and the men went to eat their breakfast.

As they were finishing their meal there was a knock at the door. Thaddeus stood in the open doorway.

"Come in friend," Eli urged.

Thaddeus stepped through the door and addressed Eli. "How is the progress on the arrows?"

"They're finished," he responded. "Follow me."

Eli led him through the house to where the arrows sat.

Looking satisfied Thaddeus asked, "How much of the potion do you have left?"

Eli held up the bottle with the remainder of the potion to show Thaddeus.

"Would you object to me taking that with me?"

The request was a surprise to Eli, but he agreed.

"Why do you want it?" Eli asked.

"Just in case," Thaddeus replied. "Not that it will make much of a difference, but I figured the more people that have access to this, the better off we would be."

"I agree, take it," Eli said.

The arrows had completely dried in less than an hour, and Eli and Japheth deposited the prepared darts into their quivers. From that point on they carried their bows with them everywhere, they would not be without them.

The morning passed quickly, and just before noon yelling was heard in the distance. Those in the town closest to the noise looked to investigate. One of the watchmen outside of the town was hollering and sprinting towards Licentia.

Suddenly from out of the forest came a blinding light. It struck the running watchmen, who fell limp to the ground.

A horn blew a deep, loud foreboding sound. It was audible to everyone in Licentia. A few moments later it blew again. There was utter and complete silence in the town, and in the surrounding forest. Two figures emerged from the forest and moved deliberately towards the town. About halfway between the forests edge and the burnt remains of the town wall they stopped.

Crag's low, strong voice broke the silence.

"People of Licentia, before you stands the most powerful man on earth, the great Vesuvius. He has it within his power to destroy this place in an instant, but he mercifully extends to you an opportunity. He desires to face your champion, alone. If he accepts and presents himself now, Vesuvius will destroy this town in a flash once he is triumphant. There will be no suffering or anguish. He will make your end quick and painless.

"However, if his challenge is not accepted, you will all die slow, agonizing deaths. You will suffer in ways you cannot imagine.

"The choice is yours. You have only a few moments to decide."

Panic began spreading throughout Licentia. Crag was close enough to the town that most could tell that he was impressively huge, and not fully a man. This fact, coupled with the challenge, and accompanying consequences, put fear into most of the town. The people were moving away from where Vesuvius and Crag stood. Japheth, his family, and a few brave others made their way against the stream of people towards them.

Japheth was resolute in his mind. He would burst past the wall and bravely meet his destiny, whatever it was. When he was only a few steps from the wall he was grabbed from behind. It was his friend Thaddeus.

"Japheth, you can't go out there alone," he pleaded.

"I have to, for everyone's sake."

Thaddeus countered, "Isn't there any way to hide or conceal someone so that they could go with you?"

The question helped Japheth remembered making his horse invisible. At the same moment, Eli was at his side, about to dissuade him as well.

Japheth looked at the two men that he most respected in this world. "I do have an idea. Remember when I made only my horse invisible. I may be able to do that again, but it takes a lot of concentration and I'm not sure how long I could maintain the spell."

Eli broke in, "Can you do it to both of us?"

Japheth didn't respond verbally. He closed his eyes, held out his hand, and uttered the spell. When he opened them his father and friend had vanished. The surprise of success broke the spell and they reappeared.

"I guess that answers that," Thaddeus replied.

"Could you keep that up for long?" Eli asked.

Japheth was troubled in his answer, "I'm not sure."

From outside the wall Vesuvius bellowed. "My patience grows short. Will you face me or not?"

Japheth responded to his father's question. "I will try. Stay in front of me so that I can focus on you. I may have to move slower than normal so walk slowly."

"Son," Eli interjected, "when it is time to fire on Vesuvius, we must do our best to do so at the same time. I think if we fire together, we will have a much better chance of hitting him with at least one arrow. You do what you have to, and I will try to time my shot with yours."

"Agreed," added Thaddeus. "And if he is not hit, I will take it upon myself to get the potion on him."

"It's not much of a plan, but I'm afraid it's all we can do."

"Son, no matter the outcome of this day I am proud of you. You have not shrunk from the challenges before you, and if that is all that a father can teach his son, that is enough."

"I love you father."

"I love you too son."

Eli and Thaddeus positioned themselves in front of Japheth. He closed his eyes, spoke the spell, and reluctantly opened his eyes. As expected, they had disappeared.

They walked out slowly from behind the wall. Japheth kept his eyes forward, always fixed on Vesuvius, and whatever it was that was next to him. He gripped his bow in his left hand. His right he kept by his quiver, ready to grab for arrows at the first opportunity he could. He could see the grass on either side of him flatten where his father and Thaddeus' feet were setting. He hoped it would be imperceptible to Vesuvius. When he had gotten about thirty yards from Vesuvius he stopped.

"It's nice to see you again, boy," Vesuvius sneered. "You think that by being brave you will have at least spared your people a great deal of suffering. You are mistaken. I will not show mercy to them. I only wanted you to face me so that you would know that you did not defeat me, that you will not be victorious, and that I will find the most innovative of ways to inflict the most pain and suffering that I can on this town. Licentia will serve as an example to the unconquered world of what will happen if I am challenged. There are ways to inflict suffering that you cannot even imagine."

Japheth defiantly cut Vesuvius off. "Did you learn them from Godun?" His words startled Vesuvius. He could see that he had caused a level of uneasiness in him.

"How do you know of Godun?" Vesuvius inquired.

"I went in search of his book."

Vesuvius measured Japheth up, not knowing whether or not he could trust his words. "Which book would that be?"

"The one he took to the mountain," Japheth answered.

Vesuvius looked at Lux. "How did you leave with your sword? He would not have let something that powerful slip through his fingers."

Japheth looked into Vesuvius' eyes confidently. "I defeated him."

Vesuvius laughed, yet there was a hint of worry in it. "You could not defeat a wizard such as him. His knowledge and skill eclipse my own."

Japheth was feeling bolder. "Yet here I stand, with the knowledge that he exists, and the sword in my possession."

Vesuvius was growing increasingly uneasy, but before he would allow himself to doubt, he looked at Crag and motioned his head towards Japheth.

Crag rushed Japheth. As he did, he let out something that was a mix between a yell and a roar. The sudden charge and the alarm caused by his bellow caused Japheth to lose his concentration and he could no longer keep his father and Thaddeus invisible. They appeared instantly.

Vesuvius cursed.

The two men's sudden appearance startled Crag, but he continued charging. Thaddeus had already drawn his sword and he moved to intercept Crag. He brought his sword down hard over his head, but Crag simply turned his head, and Thaddeus' sword came down on his horn, with no noticeable damage. Crag sent a powerful fist into Thaddeus' chest which drove him to the ground.

Eli had pulled three arrows from his quiver and released them in quick succession.

Crag saw the motion from the corner of his eye and lifted his arm to intercept the first arrow, which sunk into his forearm. He dropped his head to dodge the second, and he caught the third. He grabbed the arrow in his forearm between his teeth and savagely ripped it from his arm.

Although Eli had not seriously injured Crag, he had made the beast change his mark. Crag charged and was upon him before he could gather more arrows from his quiver.

Eli stood his ground until the last moment. When Crag ducked his head to ram Eli, he dropped towards the ground and put his shoulder into Crag's knees.

Crag swiped at Eli and he flew tumbling over him. He hit the ground and rolled several times. He was on his feet quickly, but so were Eli and Thaddeus, swords drawn.

Crag drew his own massive sword and a knife from his waist and moved towards the men.

Eli and Thaddeus hacked and slashed at the monster before them. The speed with which Crag moved was startling. As the men attacked, they fared well if they kept Crag on the defensive, but when Crag attacked his quickness was surpassed only by his power. His first strike nearly knocked Eli off his feet.

In the midst of the swordplay, Crag took advantage of an opening and kicked Thaddeus hard in the shoulder. The brutal blow sent Thaddeus to the ground bleeding, sword dislodged from his hand.

With Thaddeus down Crag turned his full attention to Eli. It was all Eli could do in his hobbled state to fend off the violent attacks. He used his sword defensively and moved his body away from the barrage of strikes. Crag was fast but predictable.

Somehow during the onslaught, he noticed Japheth reaching for arrows. He knew he must fire at the same time as Japheth if they wanted to increase their chance of success. In a brash move, he blocked Crag's knife with his sword, crouched under the slash of his sword, and rolled between his legs. As he did, he dropped his sword, and grabbed his bow and three arrows, the metal one included. He rose and drew his bow in one smooth motion and prepared to fire on Vesuvius.

As he rose, he saw Thaddeus directly to his right. He heard the animal scream of Crag as Thaddeus drove his sword into his side.

Eli released one arrow, two arrows, then the third, special arrow.

Time seemed to slow for Eli. Vesuvius looked to be nearly ten feet tall. He had been preoccupied with Japheth's arrows, as each arrow was turning to ash as it neared Vesuvius. He could see that Japheth had fired his arrows sooner, and he watched as Japheth's metal arrow was deflected by Vesuvius' staff, shooting past him into the meadow.

His focus now fell to his own arrow. He observed Vesuvius noticing his arrows as they turned to ash, and his metal arrow nearing Vesuvius' shoulder. Vesuvius spun backward and fell to the ground to avoid the arrow, which like his son's, fell harmlessly into the grass.

Crag grasped Thaddeus by the wrist and flung him out into the meadow. He turned to face Eli who was swiftly backing away from him and grabbing for his last three arrows. Crag grabbed the sword and painfully pulled it from his side. Thick dark blood ran from the open wound. He threw the sword to the ground and let out an animal roar, then charged.

Eli fired his three arrows quickly. Crag caught the first arrow, then the second with his other hand. The third found its way into his arm as he raised it to stop it from hitting him in the neck.

Eli backpedaled. He was totally defenseless. He had dropped his sword so that he could fire the arrows at Vesuvius, and now he had nothing in his hands to defend himself with.

Crag picked up speed. As he neared Eli, Japheth noticed his father's predicament and shot an inpulsa spell at Crag. The spell engulfed him but did not have the expected effect. It did hinder him slightly, and he tripped over his own feet, falling to the ground. His head violently struck one of the few large stones in the meadow, briefly stunning him as he slid to a stop at Eli's feet.

Eli took two steps forward and kicked with all his might. His foot hit Crag in the jaw, and his head dropped.

Eli moved as quickly as he could to Thaddeus who was wearily getting back on his feet.

"Thaddeus," he said, "me and Japheth both missed."

Thaddeus nodded in understanding, no more needed to be said. He moved towards the forest, staggering as he went.

Eli picked his sword off the ground and readied to face Crag again. Crag stood, hunched over and shook his head to clear it of the fog.

He looked at Eli with chilling rage in his eyes. He stood fully upright, and for the first time this battle, he stumbled.

Eli saw his window of opportunity and he attacked. He swung his sword desperately. Despite his best efforts, Crag was still too quick for him to land a blow. Crag weaved, spun, and dodged out of the way of each of Eli's attacks.

Eli thrust his sword at Crag, and it sank deep into his stomach. Crag reached out and grabbed Eli's sword hand at the wrist. His other hand came crashing down in a steel fist that caught Eli squarely in the side of the head. Eli went to the ground, face down and dazed.

Crag, with the sword still in his gut, put a huge hoof on Eli's back and began applying pressure. He continued until he heard ribs crack and break, and Eli cried out in pain. He reached down, turned Eli over, grabbed him around the neck with one massive hand, and lifted him off the ground.

Eli swung both fists, one after another, in quick succession. Each blow landed on Crag's face, but he was largely unfazed by them, so much so that he made no attempt to stop him. Eli stopped momentarily. Crag looked at him, contempt in his eyes, blood coming from his mouth and said, "Is that all you can do?"

Eli began swinging his fists again. After a few blows from each hand, he smoothly swung his right hand down and grabbed a throwing knife sheathed in his belt. His left fist landed. When his right came around again, he lodged the knife in Crag's neck.

Crag grimaced. Then he cocked his head to the side and planned to slam a horn on Eli's head. Crag pulled Eli in and moved his head forward, a massive horn moving towards Eli's vulnerable face. At the last moment, Eli maneuvered his arm between his face and the curled horn. As it struck his arm, then face, Eli heard a sickening crunch, and pain filled his arm and head. His vision swirled and began to fade. The last thing he remembered was falling to the ground, and Crag's crippling weight landing on top of him.

CHAPTER 29

Thaddeus moved towards the tree line. He knew he had to get close to Vesuvius to get the potion on him. He thought if he moved just inside the trees that he could move around behind him and sneak up close enough to touch him.

Thaddeus moved quickly despite his battered body. The beating he took from Crag made his entire body feel sore and broken, yet he pushed on.

Once inside the trees, he moved around and positioned himself behind Vesuvius. He knew he would need to wait until Vesuvius was totally preoccupied to be able to get close enough. He took his position behind a large tree and waiting for his opportunity, coated his knife with the potion.

⟫⟪◍⟫⟪

After Vesuvius cursed, he muttered a spell. It was one he had learned in one of the books Godun had collected from a wizard family, the spell was used to make plants or animals grow. Upon experimenting with it he found that it would work on himself as well.

Japheth stood in utter shock as Vesuvius grew somewhere between nine and ten feet tall.

Vesuvius stamped his foot on the ground and a small mound appeared and moved toward Japheth. He remembered the story of the encounter with the messengers and knew what was coming. Japheth dove to his left and rolled just in time to avoid what looked like a ball of lightning as it exploded from the ground and passed through where he had been standing.

Wanting to frustrate Vesuvius, he guessed at the spell he would cast next. Japheth knew that Vesuvius had a fascination with fire, so he uttered the spell to counter the ignis spell.

Vesuvius' outstretched hand had just begun to produce the magical fire when the spell fizzled and only produced a small wisp of smoke.

Embarrassed and enraged, Vesuvius moved towards Japheth. Vesuvius brought his staff down. Japheth quickly cast the clipeum spell and the staff smashed furiously into it. Japheth could feel the reverberation it caused. It was almost as if the force of the blow could break through the spell.

Japheth targeted the staff with the conglacior spell. It had only a few moments to work before Vesuvius noticed that it was getting cold. He uttered the counter spell.

Japheth spoke the impetus spell. A mighty gust of wind came from nowhere, with the added power from Lux, the spell made Vesuvius stumble backward and fall.

Japheth then used the ignis spell but was too slow. Vesuvius easily countered the fire. Japheth noticed that Vesuvius' increased size had made his movements slower, something he hoped to take advantage of.

Vesuvius reached out a hand and curled his fingers up. As he did, Japheth found himself immobilized as had happened before. He panicked. He didn't know how to counter this spell, but he knew if he didn't do something, he had only moments to live.

In a decision of desperation, he used the festinent spell. He did not speed up, and it did not counter Vesuvius' spell, but he was able to move. His actions surprised and frustrated Vesuvius, and the spell was broke.

Japheth concluded that he would not have a better opportunity than now to hit Vesuvius with an arrow. He had frustrated him about as much as he was able, and any advantage it would give him would soon be useless.

He quickly drew four arrows and fired them rapidly, the metal arrow last. In order to get a careful aim, he hesitated just slightly on the last arrow, the crucial one. That moment of hesitation was costly. As the arrows flew, they turned to dust, except the last one. It was fired just enough behind the others that as Vesuvius noticed that it did not disintegrate, he was able to deflect it with his staff.

Japheth felt sick. He noticed more arrows coming from the direction of his father. He watched as his arrows were also destroyed, all but the last one.

Vesuvius was now watching for the same thing coming from Eli and was prepared to dodge the last arrow. He contorted himself around so he would not be struck, but as a result, he had to fall backward to the ground. The fall jarred him enough to break his growth spell, and he returned to his normal size.

Japheth dropped his bow and shucked Lux from its sheath. Quickly he drove Lux into the ground and yelled, "Occipitalis!"

A large crack in the earth opened up where Lux penetrated the ground and moved towards his foe.

Vesuvius dove to the side and narrowly missed being swallowed up by the approaching crevice. During his frantic dive, his staff slipped from his hand and landed precariously close to the edge. Vesuvius rolled, then regained his feet and dove back for the staff. As his hand neared it, the tremors created by the opening earth vibrated the staff enough that it slid down into the fissure.

Vesuvius rose, renewed hatred in his eyes. He began casting spells so quickly that Japheth could not recognize them fast enough to counter. He cast the clipeum spell and settled in behind it. One spell after another was intercepted by the invisible shield. The air began to fill with dust, smoke, and vapor. This continued for only moments, but it seemed like hours to Japheth.

Fear was beginning to overcome him, and doubts rose in his mind. Through the haze, Japheth could see Crag charging his defenseless father. He shot an inpulsa spell, the shock hit Crag but did not stop him. He saw the beast trip and fall to the ground and his father viciously kick him.

He decided to change tactics. He cast the festinent spell and felt himself speed up. Then he made himself invisible and moved quickly away from where Vesuvius was targeting his spells.

The barrage of spells stopped, and the haze dissipated. Vesuvius could not see Japheth, just the scorched earth. At first, this pleased him until he realized that the boy's body was not among the destruction.

Japheth watched as his father battled Crag. He saw Crag step on him, then pick him up by the neck. He wanted to intervene, but he knew it was more important to defeat Vesuvius. His decision tore at his heart but he turned his focus to his foe. He could not see Thaddeus and guessed that he was now all alone.

Japheth thought that if Vesuvius would be defeated it would be him, and him alone to do it. He still felt a feeling of despair, for he didn't believe he could win, but he knew he must try.

Vesuvius turned and looked to see Crag fallen to the ground lying still. He scanned the area but could not see the boy.

"Are you afraid to face me?" Vesuvius challenged. "I know you are, that is why you brought those two men with you."

"Is that why you brought that monster with you?" Japheth countered.

Vesuvius' head turned in the direction of his voice. "You think I am worried to face a boy like you? You think too highly of yourself?"

Vesuvius was trying to get Japheth to give his position away, but he remained silent and unmoving.

Japheth noticed a movement behind Vesuvius. As the looked closer he could see that it was Thaddeus moving quietly through the grass towards their enemy. He knew he must get Vesuvius' attention and hold it for Thaddeus.

He cast the conglacior spell with Vesuvius as his target. The evil wizard felt his body grow cold and he simply countered it.

"Listen, boy, do you think you can defeat me with such basic magic?"

Japheth remained silent and moved slowly, deliberately towards Vesuvius. He was getting close enough to make his move when Vesuvius disappeared. Not wanting him to move far, Japheth cast the ignis spell in his direction. The spell was countered, and Vesuvius became visible again, as did Japheth.

Vesuvius began rapidly casting spells and Japheth was forced to hide behind a clipeum spell. It had only been a few moments when Japheth saw the mound of ground in front of him explode and engulf him.

He fell back in agony. His entire body convulsed. Lux had been thrown from his hand somewhere behind him. Barely conscious he saw Vesuvius standing over him.

"And now boy, you die."

Still wanting to buy Thaddeus time Japheth spoke in a more humble and subdued tone, although his words came out as more of a whisper. "Why do you want to rule mankind?"

"Power," was his reply. "Once you taste of it you can never get enough. Ruling mankind is just part of my plan. Once I bring all men into subjection, I shall raise an army as the world has never seen. I shall lead them to Black Mountain, and defeat Godun. I will then have the secrets of eternity at my fingertips. Unlimited power will be mine, and with Godun gone no one could possibly stop me."

Vesuvius reached down, and grabbing Japheth by the neck, lifted him off his feet. "Should I crush your windpipe and watch you struggle for air until you die? Or should I use magic, something especially excruciating?"

Japheth looked at him, the defiance returning to his eyes, "How about neither."

Japheth had watched Thaddeus close the gap between him and Vesuvius, and as Japheth spoke Thaddeus drove his knife, into Vesuvius' back.

Vesuvius dropped Japheth and whirled to face Thaddeus, leaving the knife. Thaddeus took the final step between them and hunching over, he put his shoulder into Vesuvius' waist, wrapped his arms around his legs, and lifted him from the ground.

Japheth retreated and instantly found Lux. He turned just in time to see Thaddeus, nearly running while carrying Vesuvius, they both plunged into the open chasm that still remained. As they reached the edge, he heard Thaddeus yell, "For Concederet!"

Japheth watched as his greatest enemy, and his greatest friend fell into the seemingly bottomless pit.

He hurried towards the massive crack in the earth. He knelt down at the edge and peered into the abyss. At first, he saw nothing move, then just above the darkness he saw a hand reach out and cling to a rock. Then another appeared and clutched onto a root. Pulling himself up, Vesuvius looked to see Japheth peering down at him.

Japheth backed away from the pit, and with tears in his eyes he drove Lux into the ground and shouted, "Motus!" As before the ground began to rise and fall as waves of the sea. The motion of the earth caused dirt and rock to break free and fill the pit.

Japheth removed Lux, and the motion stopped. Then he sat on the ground and wept.

CHAPTER 30

Japheth got up and walked towards where his father had fallen. Abigail, Deborah, and Adam had already made their way there. Crag had been rolled off Eli.

Abigail kneeling by her husband, looked up and said, "He's still breathing."

Japheth knelt by his father and put both hands over his chest before casting the sana spell. A glowing light radiated from his hand and enveloped his father. Japheth removed his hand and his father's eyes sprang open.

Eli got to his feet before speaking, "I feel, perfect. What has happened to me?"

"Japheth used Lux's power to heal you," Abigail said.

Eli smiled, "This is incredible, I haven't felt this good in a long time."

He looked around and asked, "How was Vesuvius defeated, and where is Thaddeus?"

The family turned and looked to Japheth for answers.

Tears welled in his eyes as he retold how Thaddeus had sacrificed himself to assure that Vesuvius was destroyed.

"I'm sorry son, I know he meant a great deal to you," Eli said. "We were all fond of him. He died a hero, and he avenged his family and his town. He was a good man, and he will be missed."

The family walked back to Licentia, Eli still had a limp.

They were greeted by the townsfolk, who were in great spirits, but still showed their respect for Thaddeus' sacrifice.

Aaron approached, "I hope now we can finally live in peace."

Eli responded, "I think we can, the others that Vesuvius had brought under his control will not. He will have men ruling over them, keeping them under their submission. Once they get word that Vesuvius is no more, they will move into his spot as lord over the area. Some may be worse than he was. I don't know if it is our place or not to help them, but I think it should be offered."

"There is also Godun," Japheth interrupted.

Eli looked at him, "What do you mean son?"

"He leaves Black Mountain every so many years. He searches for books like our family has, and for artifacts like I have in Lux. After I did what I did to him I think I know where he'll be coming the next time he comes down."